Ashes of the Arena

BioDome Chronicles, Volume 1

Kenny B.Smith

Published by TeapotsAway Press, 2026.

This is a work of fiction.
Similarities to real people, places, or events are entirely coincidental.

ASHES OF THE ARENA

First edition. May 1, 2026.

ISBN: 978-1948643221 (D2D,) 978-1-948643-21-4 (AMZ)
978-1-948643-23-8 (B&N), 978-1-948643-24-5 (IS)

Written by Kenny B.Smith.

Trigger Warnings

This book includes depictions of sexual coercion, extreme medical procedures, and graphic arena violence. It also has sex scenes and adult language. Protect your peace.

To Lee - You're the one. If you know, you know.

One

Luca sat looking at the projection on the wall. His wrist ached, forcing him to get up and pace to charge the watch which projected the images. Pacing always led him to a coughing fit. Hard to concentrate when your lungs were trying to push themselves up your throat. If the air wasn't so thick with pollution, it would be easier to move around. Shoving his hand into his pocket, he counted the pills, pinching each one with his fingers. Because he had his brother as a dependent, there was no way he could possibly make them last for both of them for the next two weeks. He considered cutting them in half but that wouldn't work, even if he had twice the amount it wouldn't be possible unless he rationed them better. Without the medicine, it knocked hours if not days off their lives and they were both too young to die.

He stared at the projection on the wall again. Luca's likes moved up a little, so the video was good but not great. The likes and followers he managed to catch were enough to increase his stipend by only two Digicred, which were worth at least four Govcreds. That might get him more pills but was still not enough to last until the Govcreds paid out. It certainly wasn't enough to get him into the competition for the BioDome. He couldn't quite figure out how those people got in but then again, he didn't know how Marcus managed to get everything the government withheld for credits either.

The coughing started as he covered his mouth with his elbow to stifle it and clicked the button on his watch to clear the display. Walking down the hall, he checked on his younger brother, Warren, before throwing a pill into his mouth, biting it in half, and spit half back into his hand. Warren would get a complete pill, but Luca would have to do without. Maybe next year when his brother went from a dependent to the working class, this would not be as much of a reality. Two full Govcred incomes might get them through, but he doubted it. The government still hadn't recovered from the over-pollution scandal of 2036, when the world's creditors and allies withdrew their financing and support causing the economic crash of 2041. The world never recovered.

Luca loved history, mostly the pictures of what the world looked like then, beautiful and green. Maybe he would have a nice house on a farm, spending hours outside in the sunshine. Now he existed on the fringe, the lowest of the low. For the sake of his brother, he was determined to rise out of these surroundings, placing himself in the running for the Arena. The Arena was the most popular show on the stream today and the only national show they were allowed. The only way to get an invite was to gain a huge following with likes numbers in the six-digit category, but he couldn't seem to get his vids to go viral. Luca was desperate for the formula.

At the end of the hall, Luca spied the frail form of his mother. Looking at her now, it was hard to believe she'd managed to get through two pregnancies to produce two healthy sons. Luca's father died when Luca was young. Maybe his father was 25 but his mom was fairly young when Luca was born. Luca couldn't remember. His mother never married again but had Warren twelve years ago. They didn't have the same father. Now, at the age of 41 herself, she was not long for this existence. He figured she had another few months and there was no way to quell her pain. His mother no longer received Govcreds because she couldn't work and making videos to get likes was not an option. No one wants to see the pain of a dying woman.

For a moment, Luca wondered if he would ever get married or find someone who wanted to have children. Marriage was more for show and reliability than it was for procreating. Therefore, marriages took all forms. Luca couldn't understand why someone would want to bring a baby into this world, including himself. There was something about a partner who wanted to always be around you that he found oddly comforting.

Breathing in deep caused more coughing. Luca's eyes fell to the floor as he dragged himself to his room and flopped down on the bed. How was he ever going to get enough likes and follows for the Digicreds he needed to make it to the local Arena? Tomorrow, he would talk to Marcus and see if he could help. For now, he just needed rest.

Two

The sun rose over the gray sky, causing it to light up a shade of orangey brown. Deep reds shone across the brown clouds, which only added to the dead and dingy look of the scenery outside. The entire area smelled like rotten eggs, at least that was what people said. No one ate eggs anymore, at least no one Luca knew ate them. He had never seen a real egg, but Luca was well familiar with the smell and the look of the sky.

Pictures in books showed the sky as blue with white fluffy clouds. Those were skies he had never seen in person. In fact, he was never allowed to be outside. They were remanded to the glass hallways, so they could get their sunshine but were better protected by the special glass from the UV rays and the pollution from the factories.

Pictures from the BioDome had the same skies as the pictures in books, but they were masked by the lush vegetation and vines creeping up the sides of the walls. The sun shone in around his Block, but the Dome had fresh fruits and veggies, wonderfully recycled air to breathe and all the comforts one would love to have to live a nice, long life. People in the Dome lived to be at least a hundred, with their filtered air, natural surroundings, UV protections, and medical technology.

The Dome was the only escape for someone from Luca's Block. Those younger than sixteen had some other options because they could seek specialized training, but he was far too old to specialize now. He was doomed to shred and burn the money and papers from years past and smelt down all the coins for the metals they contained. It wasn't necessarily entertaining work, but it was different from day to day depending on his assignment.

Unfortunately, it was also toxic and without the Digicreds, he couldn't afford all the protective gear he needed . It wouldn't be long before his pollution poisoning was far too advanced to stay indoors for work. As one succumbed, the government gave you jobs outside of the glass walls and the protections those walls afforded. Scroungers rarely lasted more than a few months outside before being bed-ridden.

This was why he insisted his brother specialize whether he liked it or not and he had an affinity for the computers and electronics, both of which would keep him out of the burners and the mines even if it didn't afford him anymore Govcreds. Everyone was treated equally outside of the Dome, regardless of skills and specialization but learning specific skills allowed you access to many different advantages. Doctors had access to the stores of rationed medicine, and it wasn't unheard of for small portions of shipments to disappear. Computer companions and designers often had access to code and could change things in the system. Many botanists and scientists as well as doctors were allowed to work within the BioDome itself allowing them to breathe clean air and walk among actual plants for at least part of the time.

Luca only saw pictures and videos of things like that. Those were the ones he liked the most.

Those inside the Dome itself lived in the lap of luxury and offered Digicred for entertainment. Every one of them was wealthy beyond reason and most had inherited their wealth. Without the need to worry about the struggle, the people in the Dome decided what tasks were to be completed and where things should be extended and ultimately, who made it into the Arena Showdown.

Dome dwellers tried to put on the disguise of democracy, at least in the beginning. It was supposed to be a lottery but after the first few years, they did away with the lottery, upping the stakes for competitors. The reasoning – to ensure the contestants had the fire inside them to make the arena more entertaining. No, applicants had to make it through a local, regional, and national tournament before entering the BioDome finals. Everyone else was forced to watch by default as there was only one stream available, at least to those who didn't know how to hack the system.

Hackers were criminals of the highest order, guilty of treason against the state, and when caught, which was rare due to their own set of skills, they were often sentenced to death without a trial. There was no due process here, only the popular vote. Black market Govcreds, medicine, and, as Luca hoped, likes and followers were in high demand and short supply.

It was easy to let your mind wander during long days at the Burners, but Luca had allowed it to wander for too long and almost missed the call for the end of his shift. As he worked his way back to his quarters, the thought of traitors brought his mind back around to Marcus. People like Marcus kept the world spinning in a different way, where scandal and exchanges were the currency. He had no need of medicine, but Luca never understood why. Today, Luca would appeal to Marcus for help, which would be dangerous and difficult.

To find Marcus, Luca would have to go outside.Luca's chest tightened at the thought of having to choose between food and medicine for the three of them. A pit dropped in his stomach and his features distorted in the pain and anguish in anticipation of the decision in just a few days. These thoughts forced him forward with his plan.

Today, he planned to video himself risking his longevity for a trip outside the Block. If he didn't get caught or give up where he found Marcus, the video should garner more success than his last one as people would not believe he had the gall to risk his life for the sake of likes and follows, telling Luca the real currency had nothing to do with credits. Videos of the outside were rare and worth every effort. If he could catch a sunset or sunrise, this would make the risk worth it as these were the rarest videos on the stream, always garnering likes and follows in mass.

Maybe he didn't need Marcus. If this was his plan, Luca may be able to gain the following he needed on his own. Then again, it was one video and people were fickle. He would have to come up with something equally great every day this week to keep his following. Unsure of his abilities to continue to wow an audience, he vested his odds back into Marcus.

Grabbing the old and brittle breathing mask from something his mother termed, "The destruction of the world," he headed toward the recessed doorway leading outside. This one door in his wing did not have an alarm, which seemed odd. Luca assumed someone deactivated it long before they moved into these quarters,but he couldn't know for certain. He remembered being pulled from this doorway when he was younger.His father was so afraidof the effects living here would have on him. Now Luca understood his father's concerns, who hadn't lived past 35, commonplace for men without specialization. Luca refused to resign himself to the same fate despite having no acclimation for any skills.

Placing the mask and taking a deep breath, he pushed the door open. Pullingthe extra shirt from his pack, Luca tucked in between the frame and the door, keeping the door from completely closing and locking. Hopefully, no one would notice. If someone pulled it out, he would be stuck out here until one of the transports came back in the evening, but his absence would be noticed at work and at home.

The sun was starting to dip down below the horizon. He knew his chance was now if he ever had one. Racing along the wall so as not to be seen by the guard, Luca moved into an open space where you could get to old city streets and buildings. A daring photo from here would definitely catch attention and as long as it was only one, the guard would leave him alone too. Using his watch, he moved back toward the cracked and faded pavement, snapping a dozen photos in quick succession as the sun began to drop, turning the sky an unusual color somewhere between burgundy and burnt orange.

Stumbling backward off a curb, he caught himself luckily without injury. Snapping two dozen more shots, he watched as the sun made it mostly down. Now he could walk along the ruins without being caught. Darkness was the only way to hide from the guard. Pulling a sheet of paper from his pack,he followed the instructions someone had given his father years ago. It took almost an hour to get to the old warehouse.

Luca looked at the amazing sight. The tiny warehouse was dwarfed by the large BioDome behind it. He could actually see green plants inside it as the glass reflected what little moonlight one could see through the discolored sky. The Dome dominated the horizon on this side of town, stretching as far as Luca could see in either direction.

When he was little, he didn't remember it being this big, but he did hear you could get on construction crews to make the BioDome bigger. Though he'd often wondered if that were the case, why didn't everyone get to live inside?

Luca shook his head at his own ridiculous thoughts. Recovering from the awe, breathing in hard, he continued to the warehouse's doorway. There were dim lights on inside, but not enough to prevent most of the place from being blanketed in darkness. If he remembered, he was supposed to follow the lights overhead, the ones he could see were lit. His steps echoed as he proceeded up the concrete steps onto the second floor.

"Hello?" Luca's voice bounced off every hard surface. "Hello?"

Some parts of the concrete floor had holes where the rusted rebar was clearly visible.A few holes were big enough for an entire group of people to fall through. Others you couldn't see until you were right in front of them. Luca maneuvered through the maze of obstacles carefully, arriving at yet another staircase to take him up to the third floor.

Arriving at another landing, Luca grabbed his flashlight off his belt. It was too dark now for even the tiniest hint of light to make a difference.

"Hello?" he called out again in desperation.

Worry filled his chest as the thought this was no longer a meeting spot or tradingpoint crossed through his mind. Panic welled up, choking him.

"Shhhhh!" someone whispered. "Don't be so loud. The sensors may hear you and attract the guard!"

Luca slapped his hand over his mouth as he moved toward where he thought the voice came. He reached a wall and no one appeared to be hiding around it. The echo in this room was hard to track, and, in some ways, Luca imagined that very reason was the logic behind the choice. Hard to be caught if you're chasing echoes.

"Over here, dummy!"the voice whispered again.

This time, they flashed a light on and off to signal their location.Luca's legs tried to jump into a run, but his gut told him to take it slow and keep alert.

"I'm looking for Marcus," Luca whispered back. The light flickered two more times as if in response. "Are you Marcus?"

With no discernible response to the question, Luca moved across the room toward the location of the light. As he drew near, it flashed again, blinding him. Someone grabbed his arm. He flailed in the direction of the hand but couldn't seem to shake it. Stifling a scream, another hand clapped over his mouth.

"Shut up and hold still, stupid." The breath of the stranger was hot on his ear, but Luca refused to give up.

Struggling more against whoever had him, he whipped his head back and side to side, trying to inflict harm. The hand released his arm and for a moment, he thought it worked.Click. Click. The cold barrel now rested on his temple. With that action, he froze, raising his hands in front of him, still unable to face his attacker because they pinned Luca around his shoulders.

"That's better," said the voice. "I was hoping we could stay civil but it's clear you aren't a guard which means you're here for something specific. Tell me your business with Marcus."

Luca noticed the voice was distinctly female. Was this someone who screened Marcus' visitors? If she was his personal guard, he chose well.

"I am here to see Marcus," Luca said quietly. "You already said that. What is your business with Marcus?" the woman said.

"I'd like to discuss that with Marcus if I could," Luca replied.

The guard pushed Luca forward and he knew better than to fight with a gun in play. They arrived at another set of stairs, which they climbed slowly backward. It was all he could do to keep his balance as each foot reached up for the next tread. Luca concluded going backward was precautionary to keep him from pushing her down the stairs. When they reached the final floor, holes in the ceiling revealed the moon almost clearly visible. The guard whipped him around, catching his leg and forcing him to tumble to the floor and sending him sliding across the concrete with the sheer force of the movement. Nothing appeared to halt his progress as he headed for a hole in the floor big enough to swallow him. Desperately scrambling to catch hold of any object, his body flew over the edge of the expanse.Looking down, he saw this hole cut through every floor, and he screamed as he tumbled toward his death. Something yanked. His body lurched, hands grabbing above him, finding rebar to grasp but it wasn't necessary. It only took him one look to see his jacket had caught the rebar and like a hook, it held him dangling.

Laughter echoed above him. A quick assessment showed him he was still on the fourth floor or between the fourth and third floors. Clapping accompanied the echoing laughter as he saw the guard for the first time, standing above him shaking in amusement. He couldn't see her face; she was dressed all in black with a hood covering anything identifiable. The gun now rested on her hip and a pack on her back.

She wore gloves and was covered in fabric from the top of her head to her toes. Her clothing was loose, disguising her figure. Looking at her, he wouldn't have guessed he was dealing with a woman. Her voice was the giveaway.

"This isn't funny." Luca barked up at her. "Are you going to help me out?"

"What is your business with Marcus?" she repeated, her voice more upbeat from the laughter.

"You're not Marcus and I can only discuss my business with him." Luca insisted whilehe was struggling to find another hold. His hands found only empty air. His jacket began to tear. He reached up. "Man, you are thick, aren't you?" the woman placed her hands on her hips. "Of course, I'm Marcus. You found me here, didn't you?"

Luca started to panic as the sound of tearing fabric echoed again. "What do you mean, 'of course you're Marcus?' You're female."

"Marcus is just the code name used for the underground. Didn't someone explain that to you? Dear God, how did you even get this far?" She started laughing again.

Luca strained to pull himself up by his jacket, but he didn't have the arm strength. Every time he jolted back down, the sounds of ripping told him he was one inch closer to dying.

"It's been almost 15 years. I haven't dared to venture out before today because I need your help." Luca's voice strained from panic and exertion.

"Who brought you out here before?" she asked, kneeling down.

"My father. He came out to get help once.At least once that I know of." Luca pulled up again.

"I guess you pass the test then...for now," she said, reaching down and grabbing his wrist.

Together, they managed to get him back onto the fourth floor. "If you hadn't struggled so much, that would have been much easier,"she said, panting."What is it you think you need?"

Luca groaned as he rolled over to his knees, taking off his pack and his jacket to inspect the damage. How would he explain it? Someone was going to notice.

"Come on. I don't have all night and I'd wager, you don't either. Your window is narrowing by the second." She pushed her sleeve off her wrist to reveal her watch and her skin tone, which was tanned but not too dark.

"So, Marcus is just a name?" Luca struggled to process everything from the last ten minutes.

"Do you really have time for us to rehash this?" she asked.

"Do I get to know your real name?" Luca asked.

"Marcus is my real name, at least as far as you're concerned. If you come out here multiple times,you will probably see me changefaces many times.Rest assured, you have found Marcus."

"Fine. Is there somewhere safer we can talk?

Somewhere you can't shove me in a hole if you don't like what I have to say?" Luca rose to his knees.

Grabbing his arm, she helped him up. "This way." She motioned with her head. "We can talk back at the desk on the third floor. Don't mistake my kindness for weakness. If I don't like what you have to say, or I figure out you're a spy, I'll shoot you."

"Thanks...I think." It sounded weak,but it was all Luca could think to say.

"No problem," she said as she trotted down the stairs. "Anything I can do to help the cause."

"What cause?" he asked, watching her carefully. "Never mind." She brushed off the question as she showed him back to where the light was. "Sit, talk, convince me not to kill you."

"I need your help." Luca started.

She sighed loudly."I think we've established that. Be direct. Don't waste my time."

Luca released a slow breath. He didn't want to snap at her. She appeared to have little patience. "I need help to get into the arena...and I need some meds...for my little brother..."

"Save me the sob story!"she replied, breathing out in exasperation. "I've heard it all already. Just be honest and don't waste my time."

"They'd really be for my little brother, Warren. He's not quite old enough to work in the trades yet and I'm trying to get him to specialize. My mom is too sick to work. So, I need help."

"That sounds about right for the plea. Not that it's original. I'll see what I can do but it will depend how many Digicreds you have or the information you have to share." She chuckled as she sat casually on the desk. "Now, I am more interested in the unusual request. You need help getting into the arena? Aren't you a little old to compete?"

Luca stared at her. "There is no age limit for entry.

Only likes, follows,and Digicreds for supplies." He scoffed.

"Okay, okay." She raised her hands to indicate surrender. "Don't get snippy.So, what exactlydo you think we can do to help you?"

"Don't you have access to an entire network of stolen ID's and fake people? I need you to use them to get me more likes and follows." Luca said.

"What makes you think we would expose ourselves like that for you?" she hissed.

"Because I know you bet on the games. You all run a racket. And I can tell you, because of my age, I will be the underdog, but I will win, no matter what it takes. I guarantee you I will advance all the way to the end."

She chuckled maniacally, sending chills down Luca's spine. Raising her hands, he braced himself for the kill shot but instead, she removed her hood. Now he saw her face. She had tan skin in patches on her face too, but something happened to her. Half her head didn't grow hair, and it looked like part of her scalp had been cut open or cut off. He recognized scarring from the grafts necessary to close the wounds. Another scar ran down the opposite cheek. Her nose was crooked, and her chin looked like it was broken once but not set right for it to heal. Based on her basic facial structure, tone and what would have been mostly symmetrical features, he gauged she was once a very attractive young woman.

"This is what happens if you make it to the end. Are you prepared for that journey?" her tone was flat and serious.

Luca wasn't sure what to say. He just stared at her trying to take in what she might mean.How could fighting with a hologram do that to someone?

"Well, I'll take your proposal back to the others. The meds I can almost guarantee. But the other thing, the cost will be greater than what you can probably afford. It's too risky for it to be cheap. You've got a good start based on those photos." She nodded at his watch. Instinctively, he threw his hand over it to hide the pictures he took. "Just don't post any from different angles and don't post more than maybe half a dozen. If they think you did more than open a door and snap pics before it closed, they'll track you down. You can bet on that." He tilted his head at her and gave a slight nod to show he understood. "Come back here two nights from now. That should give us enough time to consider your...proposal."

Three

Luca sat at the desk, looking at his watch. Did two nights mean he was supposed to come back tomorrow? The instructions were a little vague. Two nights from the night he first arrived would be today but two nights from the following night would be tomorrow. He didn't want to wait until tomorrow, so he took a chance and sat waiting for her. After an hour, he was worried he might have been wrong. Then, something moved below him. Luca held his breath, moving to hide behind the desk. Voices whispering conversations he could not understand echoed up the steps along with the sounds of heavy boots. The guards were coming up the stairs. Getting caught here would definitely mean prison, which also meant he would lose any chance at making it to the Dome Arena.

Luca moved to hide under the desk, knowing it would not be a good enough hiding spot, but he couldn't just wait for his fate out in the open. This was the only furniture in the place, making it conspicuous but it was dark wood and dark on this floor making it hard to see from the stairs. The space was small and cramped, made even more so because it was pushed up against a column. As the group reached the landing, Luca heard one of them issue orders, followed by echoes of thumping boots around the room.

Holding his breath, heart racing, eyes darting around the space for a possible get away. The steps were closing in and almost to his hiding spot. Just when he resigned himself to a gun shoved in his face,he noticed a hole at the very bottom of the desk. It was only big enough for a finger to fit and it appeared to lead into the space that should house drawers, but the drawers were pushed up against the column. Sliding his finger in, the side of the desk moved. He looped his finger inside and pulled. It was a door. Smashing himself up against the opposite side of the desk, he managed to wedge it open far enough to see inside. It was a hiding hole, set cleverly in the floor.

Wiggling and twisting his body, he managed to get inside the hole and close the door.

Someone dropped down on the other side. Cramming inside the space, he realized it looked bigger than it actually was, but he needed to be patient and listen.

Holding his breath again, shouts bounced off the walls and floor. Were they going to move the desk? If they did, they would find him sitting in this hiding spot. He knew these people were great at camouflage and with that, he knew there had to be more to this hiding space. Guards weren't completely stupid and would eventually move it out of the way. He had to get out of there, which meant looking for another exit. Risking everything, he clicked on his flashlight as quietly as possible and tried to use his hands and body to direct the light downward.

Shining the flashlight as he struggled to move around the space, he didn't see any hatches and the floor seemed solid. He moved around checking the walls. The one behind him looked off but he couldn't quite put his finger on it. Shifting for a better view, he noticed a few loose bricks. Slowly,he shifted the top brick until he could maneuver the bottom one to slide it across the floor.

Unstacking the two bricks and moving them aside, he poked his head through the opening to see what was on the other side.

It housed a ladder that dropped down at least a floor, cleverly masked in what he assumed was part of the column below. The space wasn't large enough for him to crawl through with his pack on his back. He wriggled out of the shoulder strap, making the space even smaller. Then he pushed his feet through the hole and rolled over onto his stomach. As he slid, he could hear steps around him and more shouting, but the desk muffled the noises. He hoped it worked both ways.

The space was barely three feet across; his feet didn't struggle to find a secure rung. Bracing himself,he grabbed his pack with one hand and slid it through the opening, placing it back on his back. If they moved the desk, they would follow him unless he replaced the bricks. Quietly and carefully, he balanced one foot on a rung and leaned his knee against the opposite wall to steady himself.

Stacking the bricks on top of one another again, he pulled them through sideways, until part of the bricks hung over the edge of the wall. Then he spun them slowly until they were flush with the inside wall. Now, it was completely dark inside the column. Luca pushed his body back to the ladder and clung to the rungs in the blackness.

A loud crash echoed through the temporary wall.

They had moved the desk. Would they see the bricks like he did? Which way should he go? Going up meant he might be stranded. Down would be closer to the exit.

Looking down, he carefully made his way back down and kept going until he reached the floor at the bottom of the ladder.

Knowing he had traveled much further down than the first floor of the old warehouse, he chanced turning on the flashlight again to check if anyone followed him. The column was empty, so Luca turned and shined the light to get an idea of his surroundings. There was only one way to go, and Luca doubted it would take him back home. One foot fell in front of the other, he aimed the light on the ground looking for traps and obstacles. The further away he moved from the ladder, the heavier the feeling in his stomach became. This was not what he wanted or needed.

His light started to dim, which didn't make sense. The batteries in the flashlight were fresh. Luca began to run, needing to find the end before he found himself in the dark. The light flickered. Panic chokedLuca, heart beating out of his chest. Then...darkness.

Four

Luca sat on the dirt floor; arms wrapped around his knees as the tunnel grew colder. His watch had gone into sleep mode, so he had no idea how long he was stranded in the dark. Had someone at home already noticed his absence? His one day off was supposed to be his time to make vids or go shopping or the other mundane tasks they needed him to complete but instead, he was spending his day in a dark tunnel lost in a place he had never been. Swallowing down the panic, he decided to sleep. There was not much else he could do.

Luca's eyes burst open. Footsteps and voices echoed down the tunnel. These steps were lighter, not combat boots of the guard. The conversation felt more playful than someone giving orders too. His watch, still in sleep mode, told him it was not morning yet. The voices were getting louder. Luca heard them laughing. They sounded young and fun. Lights appeared on one side of the tunnel, stinging his eyes. His hands reflexively covered his face as he adjusted to the new brightness.

The steps and voices stopped.Luca tried to focus on them but all he could see were dark, blurry figures. Just like in the old warehouse building, they trained the lights on his face to keep him from seeing them clearly. He ducked his head down to save his eyes from the lights.

"Shit, you are thick!" said a familiar female voice.

"Who is it?" said a male.

"It's arena boy," the familiar voice said.

"This is arena boy? I thought you got rid of him. What is he doing down here?"the male responded.

"I'm not as easy to get rid of as you thought."Luca groaned.

"He speaks. I thought he was sleeping." said a high- pitched voice.

"I was told to meet. I came. You didn't." Luca coughed, leaning over to search his bag for more water.

"Well, he can't be a plant. He has no idea what the guard schedule is," said the male.

"Unless this is a trick. His ask was bigger than any I've ever heard. Still sounds like a trap," said the female from his original meeting.

"Or he's just that desperate," said the high-pitched voice.

"I am that desperate. I wouldn't have come out here if I wasn't. To be honest, I was expecting you to give me meds for a price and then send me on my way, not turn me over to the guard." Luca groaned as he rose to his feet. "My damn flashlight burned out and I got stuck. Can one of you point me toward home?"

The lights all clicked off in unison and the group was silent once again.Luca murmured under his breath, turning in the direction away from the group. A light clicked back on. Now a man stood in front of him. Broad shoulders and at least four to six inches taller than Luca. He wouldn't want to fight this guy.

"Just get out of my way. I'm tired and needed at home. If they report me missing and then I show back up, my ass is fried," Luca barked.

"He's definitely got moxie. Maybe he's the only one with the balls to ask for something so dangerous and large," the man said.

The female from before was now at his side."Maybe he's just a good actor." She put a hand on his shoulder. "How's the response to the pics."

Luca huffed at her, stepping sideways. Instead of stumbling, she stood with her arm in the same position as if he was still standing there. Suddenly, he realized someone was on the other side of him.

"Come on. Humor the lady." It was now he realized the voice wasn't necessarily high-pitched as much as it was extremely nasal.

"Oh, so arena boy and pic guy are the same guy. You didn't tell us that. Why'd you make it sound like it was two different people?" The man raised his chin toward the woman, who dropped her arm and made a short growl sound.

"Well, if he came back, I was going to give him the meds," she replied, annoyance lacing her tone.

"Lotta good that would do him," said the nasally one. "All seriousness. He seems resourceful. The pics. Remembering our meet up when he hadn't been there in a long time. Managing to find this tunnel. Maybe he is a trap." The man raised an eyebrow at Luca.

"If I was a trap, where is my back up? Don't you think they would have gone to the end of the tunnel by now to find you?" Luca stepped forward but when he did, the man blocked him.

"Well, given it sounds like you have some Creds to spend, answer the lady's question. How'd those pics fare?"

Luca released a loud, slow breath, looking at his wrist to see if his watch was out of sleep mode. "Fairly well. There haven't been pics like that on the feed for a longtime. So, I managed to get a few Digicreds." Luca folded his arms and tapped his toe.

"And he's impatient." The nasal voice hurt his ears being so close. "Look at the way he's trying to get out of here and tapping his toe like we're a bother."

The man reached into his pocket and pulled out a bottle. Luca recognized it as what he desperately needed. Looking down at his hand, the man shook it then looked back at Luca. Before Luca could react, the man tossed the bottle at him. Catching it against his chest, Luca felt relieved.

"How much?" Luca asked breathlessly, allowing the shock to filter through his body.

"That's like 100 pills or so. It's my entire stash. You can have them all for being so ballsy. It's the least we can do for your trouble, I guess, given all the good they actually do." The man shrugged and stepped around him, heading back down the tunnel.

The nasal one slapped a flashlight against her chest. "Those are double dose. You can bite them in half to make them last twice as long but don't forget to get pills with your Govcreds or they'll get suspicious and come looking for you. They monitor everything." She motioned toward his watch with her head and then followed the burly man.

"Wait, what about helping me get into the arena?"

The woman turned. "That's a big ask and not one we can grant ourselves. It's gotta go through the big kahuna."

"The big kahuna?" Luca said.

"Yeah, the boss man," the nasal one answered.

"We can grant small things but something as risky as that goes through the one in charge," said the burly man. "If boss decides you're worth the risk, we'll find you. Don't come looking for us. But I wouldn't be holding out any hope for that."

"Besides," the woman said. "I know you made at least a couple hundred Digicreds from those photos. Find someone to produce by agreeing to split some with them. Check the market for a maker."

With that, she turned on her heel as the others followed. "Home's back the way you came, arena boy." She waved over her shoulder toward the direction of the ladder.

Five

"Nallie, why'd you tell him to bite the pills in half?" the female asked.

"Because you know as well as I do. A full dose or half dose doesn't matter," Nallie replied in her signature nasally tone.

"Yeah, but he doesn't know that. You shouldn't give people false hope," Quinn said.

"False hope is all they have. If we want to give them real hope, we need to recruit more people, which will be hard to do if you keep lying to us and making choices on your own, Quinn," the burly man Rai said.

"Gah, why do you have to come down on me like that? I'm just trying to protectwhat few people we have," Quinn whined.

"Quit trying to justify it," Rai said. "Yeah, you're a smart cookie. Possibly the smartest one of all of us. But that doesn't give you the right to take away our choices."

"I think arena boy would make a good addition but at his age, he may not make it into the arena at all. I can see why he's desperate," Nallie said.

"Who asked your opinion?" Quinn snapped. "Both of you just back off okay.I did what I thought was best for everybody."

"That's just it. You don't get to decide what's best for everybody. Everybody gets to decide what's good for everybody," Rai said.

Quinn picked up the pace trying to get far enough ahead of them so she wouldn't have to listen. "Don't chastise me. He sounded like a spook."

"Honestly, I don't think he is. I think he's just really that desperate," Rai replied. "Whether you think it's best or not, I'm recommending we help him somehow."

"At the very least, he could definitely help with the gambling. If we knew ahead of time who would win or slant it to one side to give us better odds..." Nallie stopped mid-thought. "Even if he is a spook, we could use him to make money before we let him die."

Quinn stopped. Turning, she looked at Nallie's smirking face. "That may be a better plan than what I had in mind."

"Yeah, Nallie, you've got quite an inventive plan there. All we need to do is never take him back to the others and never reveal anything." Rai folded his arms. "This could work."

They walked through the arch into the cellar. The stone floor felt cold even through their boots. Wine lined the walls around them. Without missing a beat, Nallie grabbed a bottle, preparing to uncork it.

"What could work?"the voice boomed through the room, echoing off the walls and stopping Nallie in mid- motion. She recovered quickly, replacing the bottle and stepping away sheepishly.

Rai cleared his throat, "We'd like to make a proposal."

"You're back in record time. It's not lights out yet. You didn't do your job very well this evening," the voice boomed again.

Quinn winced at the sound."Can you just come away from the bull horn. This is unnecessary!"

Rai stepped in front of Quinn, shielding her with his arm. "The Guard raided the meet up point earlier this evening. It will be under surveillance for at least another week. Under the circumstances, it wasn't safe."

The voice no longer boomed as a figure in a hooded robe walked into view from the other side of the room. "No doubt from an anonymous tip, I assume." Quinn could feel the figure's eyes on her from under the hood, forcing her to hang her head to stare at her boots. "I suppose it couldn't be helped. You're all still young and lack a bit of experience. Did you get the info you needed? I hope the raid had a purpose."

"We know the guy is either averse to getting caught or really good undercover," Nallie said as Quinn slapped her on the shoulder and Rai tried to shush Nallie.

"Oh Nallie, how do we know that?"the figure sounded like it was smiling but Quinn and Rai knew it was more of a smirk. Their watcher always trying to trip them up and make them look bad in front of the others.To them, it seemed she hated her position.

"Well," Nallie swallowed hard. "Well...because..." the young girl couldn't seem to find the words she needed.

Quinn stepped forward, "Because he was in the tunnel. So, we met the mark we were sent out to meet tonight.That's what you told us to do and that's what we did."

"He was in the tunnel.Only one of them?" the figure asked.

Rai coughed. "There was only one of them to begin with, despite it sounding like a report on two different people. I think we misunderstood the report."

"Yes, I'm sure that's what happened," the figure said stepping in Quinn's direction. "Right, Quinn?"

Quinn's shoulders started to slump, and she refused to look up. "Right."

"Then I know you'll be clearer in your reports next time. Let's get some breakfast and we'll talk about your mark."

They all headed up the stairs to an enormous dining hall. Tables filled the room but only the tables at the front of the room were full. Maybe three dozen people were in the hall. They took their place at a table and dug into the scrambled eggs and bacon waiting for them in the middle. When their plates were full, a man sitting across the room stood up and tapped his glass for attention. He was an older man with gray hair and a wrinkly face wearing a stark white suit, complete with vest, jacket and tie. The white gleamed in the sunlight coming through the windows.

"I expect there is a report from Halstead's party.

Given their early return, I worry it is not good news," the man said.

The woman in the robe stood, giving the man in the suit a nod. "Thank you, Pyrious."

"Our report is a good one," Nallie blurted out with her mouth full, spitting microscopic egg all over the table, but she didn't stop shoveling more food in as she spoke. "We found a good mark to make some good money. Even if he is a spook. It doesn't matter. We'll just use him."

Quinn kicked her under the table causing Nallie's mouth fly open and all the food inside to fall out, landing all over the fresh breakfast in the middle of the table.

Pyrious snapped and pointed as men came out in butler's uniforms and replaced the plate as quickly as it had been soiled.

"What do you mean 'use him even if he's a spook?'" Pyrious eyed everyone at the table suspiciously.

"Sir," Rai stood up to speak. "We met a young man who would like our help to get him to the arena. We figured we might be able to help him achieve that. If we can predict his outcomes ahead of time, we can slant the house in our favor to make some money off the racket, above board and underground."

Pyrious stared at him, chin quivering. "I see. So, you think this is a good plan? And what makes you think you get to make the plans?"

"Well, sir, it was just an idea." Halstead said. "Apparently, the boy has a lot of spunk for his age. He's not really a boy from what I understand, which garners more odds in the house's favor." Her voice was smooth and even, no sign of fear or intimidation.

"I see. How many I.D.s would we have to blow in order for this to work?" Pyrious barked. "I am certain you hadn't thought of that. Let alone the personal cost if we get caught. You all know none of us can risk that. This whole idea sounds like a trap a spook would set for all of us."

"Nah." Quinn wiped her mouth but didn't bother to stand or look in Pyrious's direction. "We just take the restrictions off his feed.Just like what would happen if he managed to pass the likes and follows threshold. The difference is we just trick the computer into thinking he's already done it. No need to blow a single I.D. or step into any kind of trap." She placed her napkin gently on the table. "But of course,you weren't smart enough to think of that because you always over complicate things in an attempt to protect yourself."

The entire room went silent. Not a single gulp or clink of silverware or even a breath could be heard as they all waited for the response. Few people dared to talk to Pyrious in this way. The last one had disappeared without a trace.

"Young lady, I know you are very intelligent but don't think I will keep you around if you can't learn a little respect. I brought you back to life and I am not eager to lose that investment but if you continue to make me regret it, I will do what I have to do." Pyrious walked toward the table. "Escort them to their wing. They can take their plates with them."

Quinn stood up, kicking the chair back behind her so hard it fell over and skidded across the floor. One of the butlers grabbed her arm but she yanked it from his grasp. Standing up as straight as her body would allow, she walked to the door unescorted. Rai and Nallie looked at one another before rising and racing to catch up with her, leaving their plates behind as well. Once they were safely out of earshot, she pulled them into a doorway.

"Quinn, you really need to be more careful," Rai said.

"We needed him to approve of the plan, and you know he will approve it much more quickly now that he knows I am right," Quinn said. "It will be the only way we can buy our freedom from this place."

Rai shook his head at her and motioned for them to keep moving. "Come on. We don't want to get caught out here plotting. Time for rest."

Six

Luca pushed his way through the cinder blocks in the column. This time, when he moved his body out, he found himself on the first floor and not the third. Maybe this was how the woman got up to the third floor after Luca thought he heard her on the first. He didn't have time to waste. The watch on his wrist beeped as it came out of sleep mode and warned him he needed to get up for the day, even though he didn't have to go into the Burner today.

Looking around, the sun was just starting to crest over the horizon. Stepping out to the edge of the floor, he couldn't pass up the chance for sunrise shots. Those were so rare, people thought most of them were manipulated shots. People just drafted in the new atmosphere color over the blue portions of old pics. Most of them, you could tell by looking at the horizon line or how heavy the shadows fell on the ground. Luca knew these ones would be popular, but everyone would be skeptical of their authenticity.

As he looked around to give it a context verifying they were current pics, he saw the Guard come around the corner. Ducking down, back behind the column, he knew they would pass right in front of him at any minute.

Working to turn off his flash and sound effects,he unlatched the watch.

Holding it out around the column, he dared look only once to square up the shot. Then he pressed the button on the side multiple times and pulled him arm in, hoping no one saw. Spying around the other side of the column, the Guard was marching toward the other end of the building. When they turned the corner, he lowered himself down off the platform's concrete and ran for the cover of some old, dead bushes. With the world around him chronically brown and brittle, Luca never experienced something lush and green. He only saw those things in books when he was in school and his Nana used to tell stories of when everything started to change.

Sliding behind the bush, he tried not to slip directly into it. The noise of brittle breaking branches and leaves would give away his position. Scanning the area beyond, it appeared empty. He snapped more sunrise pics and then took off running across the field toward the buildings on the other side, praying the guard hadn't found his prop in the door.

As he approached, he found the shirt still holding the door open. Stopping again, he took an entire chip of sunrise photos from in front of the door.Then, he open edit and walked right into four members of the Guard pointing guns at him.

"Hands up!" one yelled. "Don't move!" yelled another.

"So, which is it?" Luca asked, his voice wavering as he struggled with which order to follow.

"Shut up and get down on your knees!" yelled another.

"Don't move!" he heard one yell again.

"Just don't shoot me." He tried to speak without moving his lips, but he wasn't sure they heard or understood him.

"I said don't move!" "I said get down!" "I said hands up!"

They all yelled in unison,then looked at one another. The one in front glared at the others. Turning back to face Luca, the man raised a hand which Luca took as some signal to those behind him.

"Put your hands up and drop to your knees. Then don't move!" the man commanded. Luca acquiesced without another word."Now lay down on the ground, face down. Then place your hands behind your back."

One of the men lowered his weapon and began to move toward Luca. Slamming his knee down on Luca's back,knocking the wind out of him, he cut the straps of his pack, throwing it to another guard before securing his wrists. Then he yanked Luca up to his feet and pushed him forward.

"I'm sorry. I just wanted to see the sunrise." Luca protested as they dragged him down corridor after corridor. "I know it's wrong but really, I just wanted to see the sunrise."

"Shut up, kid." The Guard at the front shouted at him again.

They arrived at the headquarter office for his block.

It was alive with activity. Most of the guards were fielding phone calls from other offices while some ran messages and still others were leaving in full gear. Sunlight exploded over the horizon, invading the room in a blinding flash.

Covering their eyes, the room went silent. Luca heard a low motor sound and watched as a sheet of black mesh rolled down over the eastern facing windows, reducing the light in the room to a setting akin to a low dim on a light bulb. Activity in the room resumed as if no one had even paused or noticed. Luca managed to turn his body to take a few more pics.

Someone whipped him back around,pushing him almost into a run and through a door. Before he could react, his hands were attached to a table as he was slammed down into a chair. Luca looked around the room. It was sterile and had a camera in every corner.If he didn't feel watched before, he certainly did now.

Two men sat across from him, hands on the table, both held stern looks.

One clasped his hands onto the table. "I am Howell and this is McGowen. He's here to help you sort out this situation. I'm here to find out what you've been up to. You can speak privately with McGowen if you'd like."Howell smiled at him sourly.

"Right." Luca smirked. "Privately." He motioned to the cameras."I think I will wait for my one contact and use that to contact someone who really has my best interests at heart."

"Well, that's unfortunate because you haven't been charged with anything thus you have no right to a contact." McGowen said.

"Then, I should also be free to leave, which means you need to release me from this table." Luca said. "Just because I didn't specialize like you lot here doesn'tmean I'm not educated."

Howell and McGowen exchanged looks. McGowen shook his head. "Okay,let's stop this right now. There's no need to get into a pissing contest here. We're all strong men. How about we start over?"

"That depends. Does starting over mean you unlatch me from this table?" Luca asked sardonically.

"I think we can accommodate that request as long as you agree to tell us what you've been up in the last twenty- four hours." Howell grimaced as he reached into his pocket for the keys to the restraints. "Agreed?"

"Sure. What do you want to know?"Luca smiled, feigning sincerity.

There was a knock at the door. Another guard entered, tossing Luca's pack on the table. Luca barely had time to pull his hands out of the way before it would have slammed down on them. He knew his pack was heavy enough to possibly cause damage. Although he tried, Luca couldn't hide the shock or dismay he felt at the action.

"Well, let's start with what we have in this thing." Howell stood up, opening the pack and shoving his hand inside.

He produced the mask. Luca had to take it off while he was running but it was his only protection from the toxic air at work. Howell placed it on the table. Then he pulled out a package. Opening it revealed snacks.Next, he tossed Luca's canteen on the table after opening it to sniff the contents then he started to open the other pockets, searching for more loot. One pocket revealed Luca's ear buds, the cord wrapped neatly.Luca eyed an old, smashed granola bar Howell managed to pull out of another pocket. With no idea how long it had been there, he could not confirm nor deny whether he placed it there. Further searching yielded no more items. Howell harrumphed loudly as he tossed the bag on the floor and plopped back into the chair. It was the first time either one of them showed any emotion.

"Okay, so let's talk about these items." McGowen motioned toward the table. "Why would you need any of this on a normal day?"

"Well," Luca picked up the gas mask. "This is for work. I work in the Burner, and the fumes get pretty thick. It helps me breathe. This, of course," he picked up the pack of food, "is because we don't really get breaks or lunches and working twelve to sixteen-hour days makes a person hungry." He grabbed the canteen, "I would think this was self-evident as I work in the Burner. It gets really hot in there. So, I'll let you use your imagination. While these," he grabbed his ear buds, "Provide some semblance of entertainment for the boring job of watching things burn and melt all day." Luca flicked the ear buds back on the table, leaned back in the chair and folded his arms.

"And this?" Howell prodded the old granola bar. "Not sure. I may have put it in there at one point, but I honestly don't remember. It could be from my brother or my mother trying to help me with snacks while I'm working. It could have been in the bag when I inherited it from my dad." Luca sat straight-faced and sighed. "I suppose if that's my crime, not remembering where the old granola came from, then I am guilty."

"You were coming in from outside. What responsibilities take you outside?" Howell scowled at him.

"Well, I've decided to become a nature photographer. It's garnering a lot of support as a movement and now, I may just make it to the arena." Luca said triumphantly, although he didn't realize he'd sounded so smug until Howell pounded a fist on the table.

"There is no such things a nature photographer. You're not supposed to be outside. It kills you faster." Howell demanded.

The smug look fell off Luca's face as he watched McGowen straight arm Howell to keep him from jumping over the table. Luca swallowed hard. They were being more serious about this than he thought they should. Perhaps they had seen him at the warehouse ruins.

"Are you certain you were only just outside the door taking pics?" McGowen's eyes narrowed as he waited for the answer.

"Where else would I go?" Luca asked, leaning forward and trying to seem more casual.

"I don't know.Why don't you tell us?" Howell seethed.

"I'm not sure what you're getting at. I was outside taking pics. I didn't want to miss the sunrise, so I'd been out there a long time. You'll have to excuse my ignorance as I have no control over when my watch goes into or comes out of sleep mode. So, gauging sunrise can be a little tough." Luca said, using his hands expressively, hoping he was selling his lies well.

"So, you didn't end up in the south district by the Dome?" McGowen asked.

"Which way is south?" Luca cocked his head sideways as he asked the question."I've seen the Dome out the windows, but it looks very far away. How long would it take someone like me to get there? Clearly, I'd be on foot, I imagine. Would there have been enough time?"

The guards eyed him closely, unsure if he was talking to himself or them. All his questions went unanswered as they waited for a response. Luca wasn't sure how to respond so he continued to babble about math he didn't know and how much time he was outside even though it was hard to get an exact time.

"Oh, shut up!" Howell finally shouted as he stood up and kicked the chair backward out from underneath himself. "Just tell us what you've been up to."

"I told you. I have decided to take up nature photography at a very high risk to myself. People seem to really like the photos. Don't believe me?" Luca grabbed his wrist and removed his memory chip. "The pics are on there. Bring them up. You'll see."

McGowen took the chip from his hand and load edit into a drive attached to the bottom of the table on the guard's side. The pic appeared in three dimensions floating above the table.As McGowen tapped the table, the picture changed. After looking at two dozen of them, the last two dozen Luca had taken from the corner of the building and then right outside the door, he clicked it off and handed him back the chip.

"Those are some very impressive pics, but they are also as illegal as you can get." McGowen said. "Despite your talent, you should not be outside."

"If I promise never to do it again, will you please let me post them? I am well beyond my youth and trying to get into the arena. I need every advantage I can get."Luca pleaded with them.

"It can't hurt to let him post them, but we'll be watching your feed. So, you better not post any more of these nature pics or we will have no choice but to detain and charge you."Howell stipulated as he picked up the bag from the floor and chucked it at Luca. "Now get your stuff and get out of here. I don't want to see you in here again."

Luca used his arm to sweep everything off the table and into the bag in one motion. "Do I get new shoulder straps?" he asked.

"Cost of your nature photography. See if your mother has some thread handy but it will never hold things the same." Howell smirked at him.

"We're serious, Luca. No more nature shots. You understand?" McGowen rose and walked toward the door, swinging it open.

"I understand." Luca said, bowing out of the door.

Seven

Quinn flopped onto her bed and stared at the ceiling. Back in the day, Rai had managed to borrow a maintenance ladder to paint stars in the tray ceiling. If only they really glowed in the dark, she would never leave her room. Sighing loudly, she heard her stomach grumble. Looking at her watch, she knew she could sneak into the kitchen, and Lila would give her something to eat, despite it being against the rules. It seemed odd Pyrious had rules when he refused to follow the law himself.

Pyrious ran the underground gambling racket. He was trying to get bigger stakes in the above-board gambling racket of the arena as well. So far, he'd managed to get a small stake only and this made him angry. Quinn puzzled over why he would want to be a legit gambling manager anyway as he made so much more money in the illegal rackets he ran. Maybe he just wanted to appear to be part of the upper echelon of society and you couldn't get there doing things under the table.

Quinn remembered the day she came here, fresh out of the arena. Pyrious had been her sponsor, not that she needed one. Sponsors were meant to level the playing field inside the arena and they were completely optional,but she didn't realize seeking a sponsor would mean he would own her. The day she signed the contract for his support, and he explained everything to her, she thought she'd die long before any of the clauses in the contract could be enacted.

"There are existences worse than death, you know." Pyrious slithered in her ear.

If only she knew what that meant then or listened to others when they told her not to sign. It seemed a shady practice, and she was smart enough to see that, but she needed the advantages a sponsor could give her. Rounds she wasn't forced to compete. Less opposition when she might be in a draw situation. The money for gear and tricking out her avatar.It seemed so easy and reasonable at the time.

The knock at the door took her by surprise. Halstead entered through the double doors.

"I trust you managed a few hours of rest?" Halstead stepped into the room and closed the door.

"It's not time to go out again. Is he looking to be escorted to another party?" Quinn groaned.

"Pyrious is a man of insatiable needs on occasion, which is why he is so successful. You would do well to align yourself with him instead of challenging him so often." Halstead said gently as she opened the wardrobe to pull out a gown.

"He would do better not to try anything if he wants me to work with him." Quinn replied. "Besides, all my beauty was lost for the sake of the arena. Why he wants me now makes no sense."

"With a little work, if you allowed it, your beauty would return." Halstead pulled out a sparkly, skintight gown with a plunging neckline and laid it out on the bed. It's red fabric shimmered in the falling sunlight. "Besides, it's not that bad as long as you allow yourself a little enjoyment. You may be surprised. He is actually very talented."

Quinn made a face to express her disgust. "Then why does he have to buy women?"

"Pyrious hates the idea of traditional relationships. They bore him and he knows what he wants and when he wants it. He prefers no strings attached." Halstead said.

"A contract would indicate there are strings." Quinn replied trying not to gag. "So..."

"No, a contract implies there are rules for contact and separation. Therefore, it is all made simple by setting up the expectations in the beginning. Save yourself from the dark side of it all and just submit."

Quinn grimaced and shook her head.

"And if that is not enough to sway you, Quinn, you know you signed a contract and he will see it through." Halstead hung her head and became timid. "There are things worse than death, dear and Pyrious knows how to inflict it all. Don't make this harder on yourself than it needs to be."

"It's been years.Years. How can he possibly think I will ever..." Quinn couldn't finish the sentence.

"Because you signed a contract and by that, I mean, he doesn't need your permission." Halstead set her hand on Quinn's, prompting Quinn to look at her. Halstead's eyes were soft but full of pain and anguish. "He has been kind to wait for you to be ready. Patience and kindness he has not shown others in your position, but his patience is wearing thin. It's no longer a matter of when you're ready. It's a matter of when and how he decides you must be if you continue to refuse him. I speak from experience. Make it easier on yourself."

"Why? So, when you get thrown out or die, I can take your place while he replaces me with someone who is what I used to be?" Quinn broke the bond Halstead was trying to keep between them, yanking her hand out of Halstead's grasp and shaking her head. "No. I only have a few more jobs until my debt is paid in full with interest.He can't hold me here past that."

"One of the reasons his patience is running thin. You're a smart girl but even you know he'll never allow you to pay off your debt. Maybe you forgot the clause about room and board costs?" Halstead tried to get Quinn to lock eyes with her again, but she could see it written on Quinn's face.

Quinn had forgotten everything about the cost of room and board. She had been here for five years and not taken it into consideration. Jumping up, she raced to the desk, yanking open the drawer and pulling out the stack of papers. Scanning them quickly, she found what she needed. If she had succumbed when he first propositioned her, there would have been no room and board as long as she continued to submit. But she hadn't and now it was five years of room and board costs. Tears stung her eyes. Turning her head as far from Halstead's concerned glance as she could, she tried to dry them without success.

When she turned back around, Halstead had already walked back to the door. "Just give my words some thought." She opened the door and stood in the threshold. "You best begin to prepare. He's expecting you soon. It's the welcome banquet for the new contestants."

Halstead disappeared as the door followed her, closing securely. Quinn threw the papers. They fluttered elegantly all over the room as they drifted to the floor. She wanted to scream and cry. Mostly, all she wanted was to run but she knew she couldn't. Feeling her neck and the scar reminded her she could always be found. Tracked like a pet in the twenty-first century. Halstead was right. She should have just given in at the beginning. Then maybe she would have her freedom. At this rate, her freedom would never come. Maybe she could use her leverage to renegotiate her contract. That was something she hadn't tried before, but she knew it was highly unlikely he would negotiate over her submitting to him completely, whatever that may entail.

Walking back to her bed, she fingered the dress. It was soft silk. In her youth, she wished to be able to wear something this beautiful and luxurious which is what drove her to be a contestant in the first place. Now, she wondered why she ever thought being elegant and living in a bubble were a good thing. Tonight,she would try to renegotiate. Tonight, she may manage to get her freedom within her grasp.

Eight

Quinn learned a long time ago how to walk in these tall shoes, but it didn't make it easier,and it didn't keep her feet from hurting for days after one of these events. She practiced in her room to perfect her stride in the tight dress. The neckline dropped almost to her belly button and her breasts almost popped out as she walked. None of which was helped by the equally plunging back. Knowing Nallie would be able to fix it all, she was a stylist and make-up magician, it didn't bother Quinn enough to mess with it.

Nallie squealed as she walked through the door. "Lady, you look fabulous. Now turn." She motioned with her finger for Quinn to spin. Quinn grunted in dismay but indulged her, nonetheless. "Now strut." Nallie motioned again with her fingers and Quinn followed orders. "Okay, there are just a few things we need to fix to make sure you don't get a ticket for public indecency and of course, we will make all those scars disappear. Sit down. Let's get started." Nallie clapped her hands and picked up her bag of supplies, bringing it to the vanity across from Quinn's bed.

When Nallie was done, Quinn barely recognized herself. Now she was taped and pulled and pushed and concealed and... and... and... she ran out of things to describe the experience. Now her head was silent. As Quinn gazed at herself in the mirror, she watched Pyrious walk through the door behind her reflection. He came up behind her, placing his hands on her shoulders.

"You are breathtaking." He leaned in and kissed her on the bald spot on her head.

"We just need to place the wig." Nallie smiled, pushing herselfup to Pyrious and fingering his tie. "Then the look will be complete."

"You realize you could look this beautiful all the time. If you just let my surgeons work their magic on you. Quinn, you would be such a sight to behold, we would rule the Dome together."

Quinn felt herself throw up a little in her mouth at the thought of them together. "I don't know. I kinda like my scars. They remind me of where I've been. That not everyone who is beautiful is perfect."

Pyrious kissed Nallie on the hand. Then he wrapped a hand around her waist and whispered in her ear. When he released her, she smiled and pranced around Quinn, reaching for the wig.

Pyrious raised a hand, "No. No wig tonight." He smiled at Quinn. "You are right, my dear. Withoutthe wig, your beauty is bolder. More authentic. Maybe you will consider the surgeons if they make you look like this." Quinn looked pensive, considering the offer as Pyrious leaned into her ear. "In fact, I would be happy to do anything to make you more amenable to me, I'll remake you however you choose."

A cold shiver ran down Quinn's spine as she realized what he meant. Did he really think the problem was she didn't think she was beautiful? She tried not to scoff.

"Since you are ready...Nallie, I need your help with something in the bathroom."

"Sure, whatever you need." Nallie smiled and skipped back to Pyrious.

Quinn started to stand. She could clearly see into her bathroom from the mirror and Pyrious knew this, but she was in no mood for one of his shows. He pushed her back down into her chair.

"You will wait here for Rai. This won't take that long," he winked at her, then wrapped an arm around Nallie's waist, enabling his hand to grope her behind and lead her to the bathroom.

Quinn rested her hand on her forehead as they geared up for intercourse, Nallie's nasally moans rippedinto Quinn's ears like nails down a white board. She knew Pyrious wanted her to see and watch everything. Nallie straddling him from the counter. Pyrious pressing into her rhythmically, but Quinn just couldn't watch, and he knew she wasn't because he could see her face in the bathroom mirror.

While she tried to avoid any attempt to see the show, Rai had slipped into the room and now stood beside her. "You know, he'd quit putting on a show for you if you just relented." Rai said, taking her by surprise.

"With the way Nallie just agrees, you would think she liked it." Quinn responded, elated to have something else to look at.

"Actually, he promised she could get pregnant if she let him do anything, anywhere, in front of anyone to make him look like a ripe young stud." Rai said shaking his head, trying to avoid looking toward the bathroom himself.

"She wants a baby...with him. How would that work?" Quinn looked at Rai in shock.

"She'll never get pregnant. Her physical deemed her infertile right after she first got here. He knows but he never told her for occasions like this." Rai said. "So really, this is all for you."

Pyrious's huffing gained in pace and strain as Nallie's moaning became more insistent and higher pitched. She squealed in delight just before Pyrious growled and huffed and growled again. Then, there was silence. Quinn dared to glance and saw them making out wildly as he still swiveled his hips a little. She shook her head. "He's wasting his time."

"He's trying to be decent for you which is more than I can say he's done for anyone else under his contracts. You seem to have a special hold on him. I'd use it to your advantage." Rai held out his arm, helping her rise out of the chair.

"How can he expect me to sleep with him when he's prancing his other escapades in front of my face?" She said, loud enough she knew Pyrious heard.

Pyrious came out of the bathroom,his face red and his hair ruffled. Nallie followed, fixing his hair and then skipping to the vanity to pack her tools.

"So, you are adamant about exclusivity then is it?" Pyrious focused his gaze.

"Yes, I want you to sign a contract stating you will be faithful only to me and if I catch you with anyone else, both contracts are null and void."Quinn replied stoically, looking at Nallie and then back at Pyrious.

"My dear. That would mean you would need to abandon all other duties in lieu of all my wants and desires. I'm not sure you could handle that." Pyrious chuckled, shaking his head at her.

"I'm not sure you could restrict yourself to one person for any duration making the point moot." Quinn glared at him.

"Will this get you to give yourself to me willingly?" Pyrious asked.

"What does that matter? We have a contract. You have a legal right to take what you want." Quinn probed to see where she stood.

"Oh, I know that. But the contract is only a formality. It is so important that you are willing. I don't want to take anything from you. I want you to give it to me as the ultimate act of submission." Pyrious slid closer to her, wrapping his arms around her, yanking her in close.

"The only way that will happen is if I get exclusivity for two years and all my debts are erased after those two years with no new ones incurred and I am free to live should I choose to at that time." Quinn broke from his grip and stepped back cautiously, trying not to tip herself over.

"Two years! That is a very long time to be faithful. I can't say I ever have been faithful for longer than a few weeks. But if that's what it will take, I will agree." He turned to Rai. "Escort the lady downstairs please. I have some quick business," he eyed Nallie thirstily. "Then I'll be down. Wait in the car, no matter how long it takes."

Quinn waited in the car for almost three hours before Pyrious made his appearance. Not one of them said a word as they approached the Mid-City Ballroom. A tall structure made of steel and glass, covered in twinkling lights made to emulate the stars in the sky they could rarely see anymore. No matter how many times Pyrious brought her here, Quinn always found herself in awe of the sight.

Vines strewn down the glass walls and water features made soothing sounds as the water trickled along its designated paths.The floor was bright white marble and the footings a black stone she didn't recognize. Gold architectural pieces and sculptures lined the entrance walkway. This was more decadent than any contestant attending could ever dream of seeing in their lifetime.

They would be taken aback by it all, awe struck by it all, made stupid to keep it all. She remembered that feeling but it was long gone as she felt Pyrious' hand on the small of her back escorting her through the two-story double doors.

The arena contestants looked uncomfortable in their upper-scale frocks and were clustered in one corner.

Sponsors and admirers alike approached them to hold conversations and as the night progressed, she watched them disperse into opposite sides of the room with one another, leaving one young lady standing alone.

Quinn made her way to the young woman. "Hi, I'm Quinn." She held out her hand. The woman looked clueless as to what to do with her extended hand. "How old are you?" Quinn tried but received no answer. "What got you into the games?"

The girl smiled. "My avatar is Niko and I just like to play the games and make videos. I tried to decline the invitation to come here but they wouldn't let me."

"I see." Quinn swallowed her drink down hard at the thought. "Well, they are sticklers about the rules here. Kinda sucks, I know. But you'll get through it."

Without allowing for any more conversation, Quinn bolted for the bathroom. She couldn't stand the thought of this child being forced into the games against her will, for the sake of holding to the rules. It made her sick to her stomach. Getting away to recover was her only option as she couldn't tell Niko anything about the games themselves. Quinn hoped Niko would be one of the ones who managed to escape before the beginning of the next week when the tournament started. There were always one or two who managed to disappear.

Staring at herself in the mirror, she couldn't help but allow a few tears for the sake of all the contestants. Not one of them knew the depth of what they had signed up for. They had been secluded for over a month in the training center. The outside world had mostly forgotten them. Whatever happened to them now no longer mattered.

She heard the door open. Pyrious had his back to her, locking the door. Walking up behind her, he grabbed her hips and began to grind into her. It took every ounce of her energy to control her natural reaction to him. She removed his hands and bumped him back, placing a hand on his chest to keep him at arm's length.

"What are you doing?" she asked.

"We are alone. I have ordered everyone in the household not to allow me to do anything with them for two years..." Pyrious beganbut Quinn just shook her head and interrupted.

"You mean, you had one last go around with every female in the place and now you think I will let you have me."She pursed her lips as he struggled to get closer,but she wouldn't allow it.

"Well, in honesty,yes. Yes, I did do that, but I did also order them afterward this was the last time. So, you see, I agree." Pyrious smiled and tried to pull Quinn to him, but she stood her ground.

"Where is the paperwork?" Quinn asked.

"We don't need paperwork. You have my word." Pyrious replied with a smile.

"One, you're too drunk to be any fun. Two, your word means nothing to me without it being in writing and signed," Quinn replied.

"Oh, then I just want a taste of what I might be getting. A sample." He managed to break her hold and now held her firmly; both arms wrapped around her and both hands groping her behind. "Just a taste."

"What do you consider a taste?" she asked, struggling against his grip.

"Just a quick one, right here. No one will know." Before she could stop him, he had lifted her onto the dirty bathroom counter, placing himself between her legs. His hands dropped to hike her dress up enough to allow him room to rest his hips between her thighs comfortably.

All Quinn could think was this was not where she pictured losing her virginity. In a grubby bathroom with people waiting outside to use it. Her revulsion of Pyrious was well-founded and starting to boil to the surface. She had to stop this right now, doing the only thing she could think of. Grabbing his hands, she placed his hands on her breasts and pulled him into her chest. He began to fondle and kiss her as she slowly inched her way back off the counter. As she dropped to the floor, he pulled away and looked at her.

"That's not really a taste." And then he pulled her close and forced her to kiss him.

She didn't know what else to do but allow it to happen. He ran his hands all over her body, in places she never wanted them. When she finally broke away from his body again, she made her way to the door and unlocked it.

"There's your taste. Don't try anything else before I have the paperwork, or the deal is off." Quinn said, wiping her mouth and pulling her dress back down.

"So, until the paperwork is ready, I am a free agent, right?" Pyrious grinned.

"Yeah, whatever!" Quinn shouted over her shoulder as she marched out of the bathroom.

Quinn did not see Pyrious for at least an hour. The party had started to think he'd left but Pyrious was not one to leave a party early. She imagined he was trying to find someone or several someones to answer his appetite. All the better for her.

She found a seat against the far wall of the ballroom sitting down and take off her shoes. Pulling up the feed on her watch, she saw new photos of a sunrise trending vigorously up the local charts. The photos were posted by someone named Luca and after rolling through his feed, she saw the photos of the sunset. He was good at capturing great images. Quinn could see clearly why he was trending. It was amazing how far he had come in just a few days. If he could keep this momentum, he would be able to get into the arena by the end of next week.

"Wow! Who's posting those photos?" Pyrious was looking at the holographic projection from her watch. "They have skill. Maybe I should sponsor them."

"This is the guy we were talking to you about a few days ago. You know, the plan to make more money," she said as he sat next to her and proceeded to run his hand up and down her thigh.

"Baby, you may be right." He kissed her on the side of the head. "He's got potential. You better reach out to him because you're going to need to train him. How old did you say he is?"

"Early twenties...maybe. He didn't really say." Quinn smiled. "He's got balls. That's for sure."

"He would definitely be an underdog. No one would expect him to win and then once he does, they will expect him to lose right after. We could make a large profit off him, especially..." he leaned in to whisper in her ear. "Especially if I have my best girl to help rig things." Quinn pulled away from him a little. His hand was now up her dress, stroking her. "Oh, how I wish we had a contract, so we could celebrate together. Any chance you'll change your mind?"

"Nope." She stood up abruptly, contorting his hand painfully. He yanked it away. She continued, "We should go. I'll have to go out tonight to get in contact with him."

Nine

Luca poked his head into Warren's bedroom.Warren was fast asleep, surrounded by books. Lately, he had really taken to his studies, probably because he realized there was nothing else to do. Luca had been assigned double shifts all week because of his interrogation. It was obvious Howell and McGowen did not believe he was only taking pics and they were trying to keep him out of trouble by keeping him busy. Eighteen hours a day of work for six days meant no time to do anything really and his likes and follows were taking a little dip, which made him antsy.

Knowing he would need to be up again tomorrow to try and cram in enough pics and vids to post throughout the week, he only took another moment to check on Warren and moved into his mother's room. She coughed loudly as he entered.

"Hey, Mom." Luca sat down in the chair next to her bed grabbing the pills off her nightstand. "I see you haven't taken your meds today. Do you need my help?"

He opened the bottle and began to tip it into his hand. His mother rolled over and put her hand on his, ceasing his motions he looked up at her. She didn't speak, only shook her head at him. His eyes narrowed as he tried to understand.

"But Mom..." Luca choked down his responses as he tried to hand her a pill.

She refused it by pushing his hand back toward him weakly and rolling back over. "It's too late for me. You keep them," she murmured. "For you and Warren."

He stood up, pills still in his hand. Then he saw when she coughed, blood trickled out the corner of her mouth. She really was almost gone. His shoulders slumped a little more. It really was too late for her.

"Good night, Mom," he whispered as he walked back out into the hallway and headed to his room.

Luckily, his new Digicreds had allowed him to buy a new pack, which he slipped off his shoulder and dropped on his bedroom floor next to the small desk. Sitting down in the chair, he wrestled with the ties on his work boots, debating whether to take a shower or not before climbing into bed. Because most of his work was toxic, he was compelled to clean the grimy soot off his body. Grabbing his towel off the back of the door, he stripped off his clothes and stumbled half-coherent into the bathroom.

Returning to his room, he remembered to turn the hall light on for Warren, but it illuminated a figure sitting on his bed, forcing him to pause in his doorway.

The figure wore a red, skin-tight dress and boots but only had half a head of hair. She turned her head to face him, smirking. He recognized her, but she looked so different,he couldn't remember where he'd seen her before.

"Well, hello. I suppose I should call you Luca as opposed to arena boy," her grin softened.

Luca's eyes went wide. Now he wondered what happened to her and why she didn't look this way when they first met. Before he realized it, his mouthwash gaping. Just seeing her made him speechless.

"Seriously. Don't be one of those guys. I am the same person. I just look like I used to look...well mostly." She ducked her head and ran her hand over the bald. Then she clapped her hands loudly. "Snap out of it!"

"How...Where...I don't understand." Luca stammered. "How long have you been sitting there?"

Her grin widened from ear to ear, "Long enough to get a pretty good show. I suppose I should have said something but, well, you've got a nice body. And given your response to this," she motioned to herself, "I think turnabout was fair play."

Luca sat down, careful not to reveal anything, and put his head in his hands. "I really don't have time for this," he grumbled. "Why are you here?"

"I told you. We would find you. The boss accepts your proposal. We're going to give you a hand with the arena," she explained. "I will help train you, not that you may need a lot of training." She looked him up and down as he sat in just the towel. He responded by covering himself up as best his could with his arms and hands and turning away from her without getting up. "Obviously, we'll have to get you over being so shy. People in the arena don't fare well if they're shy." The corners of her mouth turned up again. "Working with you seems like it would be a lot of fun."

"I really don't have time to train. The Guard have me on double shifts to keep me out of mischief." He looked up at her as something dawned on him. "Wait, how did you even get in here? They've locked the place down since they caught me trying to sneak back in."

"Perks of being a citizen of the Dome," she winked at him. "And really, the perks of being smart like me. I've spent a lot of time wandering outside the walls and frankly, nowhere is as secure as the Guard seems to think it is."

"But you seem to be fine. Not poisoned by the air at all.I don't understand how that works." Luca looked her up and down and considered getting a closer look but remembered he was practically naked.

"I'll step out into the hall while you get some clothes on. That should make this conversation more comfortable. Then we'll discuss how this will work and you'll be able to get some sleep."

She sauntered across the room, keeping her eyes on him. He grabbed her hand as she got close, causing him to blush a little.

"Wait, I don't even know your name, but you obviously know mine." He released her hand and stared toward the floor. "I mean, what should I call you if we're going to work together."

She put her hand under his chin and raised his head to look up at her. "My name is Quinn, Luca. You can call me Quinn."

With her this close, he could see she was covered in heavy make-up and some of her scars were just barely visible with the way the light hit her face. Many must have thought she was breathtaking before the scars, but he liked her the way he met her first. The hint of beauty wrapped in strength and wit. It would still be hard to work with her.

This look was such a distraction. Luckily, it appeared only temporary.

He pulled away from her. "I better get dressed. We can work out the details when I'm wearing...well...something."

Ten

Quinn had not lied. She knew every nook and cranny, secret passage, and old forgotten tunnel throughout the city. After following her directions to different meetups for a week, he still managed to get wherever he wanted undetected. Luca wondered why Quinn would wait at the warehouse for people to come to her when she could clearly go to the people. Apparently, this resistance wasn't what he thought it might be or should be. Maybe, he reasoned, it wasn't a resistance at all but if that were the case, who and what had he aligned himself with to satisfy his need to get inside the Dome? Luca preferred not to think about it if he could help it.

Last week, they focused on what garnered likes and follows. Quinn helped him quickly amass a collection of pics and vids almost guaranteed to keep his status on the upswing and bring him in more Digicreds. Once this was done, he had enough material to post original things for months. So, when she called for training to continue, he felt a little baffled.

Quinn sat on an old rusty bench inside the concrete building she set up for their meeting. This was a new location, and it took Luca the better part of two hours just to get here. It must have taken Quinn half the day. Without any idea where he was, this seemed ominous and mysterious. Motioning to him, he ran to join her on the bench.

She said, "Okay, I know it seems like training should be done but now, the real work starts. Now, you learn combat. Most will go into the arena with little combat experience but that can't be you. The trick here is to learn how to make it look like you don't have experience and that you get lucky."

"That's how you have to win if you want our help and support. It has to look like it happened because of a lucky move or circumstances falling into your favor, merely by chance. Do you understand?" All Luca could do was nod as he tried to process everything she said as quickly as he could. "Now, with the material I have given you and what we have done from our side; you will rise quickly but not so quickly you draw too much attention from the officials or the stream. We wouldn't want anything to look suspicious." Luca kept nodding. "What is your problem today?" she sneered.

Luca froze. The wrong answer could end their relationship. "Well,I thought...you know...that first night in my room. It appeared you had a lot of make-up on. Is that what's happening now or..." he stared down at the ground.

He couldn't believe himself. How could he be so taken aback by her appearance? At this point, she looked different every time he saw her and maybe the differences were the issue. He couldn't understand why she would transform herself into the woman he didn't recognize in his room that night. Luca thought she was pretty the way she was when he first saw her, and she didn't need to do anything to improve. Her scars told her story, and he couldn't help wanting to know more. Thus far, she hadn't given away much about herself and he felt asking was giving the wrong impression.

"I... uh...it's a long story. We don't have time for that," Quinn snapped back at him. "Besides, you need to get past how I look and pay attention to what I am tryingto teach you."

He put his hand on hers. "No, please don't misunderstand." He paused, looking for her response. "I don't understand why you would change a thing about you. You looked beautiful that night in my room, in that dress, but it didn't feel like it was really you. The first time we met you were genuine. Every mark you have tells me about you and I find that fascinating and attractive. Why would you change it?"

He waited for her to yank her hand away, but she didn't. Instead, Quinn stared him dead in the eyes in a fierce way he had never experienced. Doubts pierced the earlier confidence, forcing his eyes back down to the ground.

"That was bold for someone so shy. I'm sorry you don't approve of what I am going through. To be honest, I don't want to either. It's a part of...well. I'm not sure how to explain what it's a part of."

THIS WAS THE MOST PERSONAL Quinn had been with anyone since the arena. She couldn't help it. Luca came from such a genuine place, she felt she could trust him with things she couldn't tell anyone else. It was uncomfortable for her to be this vulnerable after spending years protecting herself from predators. Now she yanked her hand away but only so she could turn away from him to hide the tears in the corners of her eyes.

Luca said, "I didn't mean to upset you. I guess we should get started."

Quinn sniffled and as Luca turned to face her, she knew he not only saw her distress, but truly wanted to fix it.

"Really, we can get started."

"It's okay," Quinn muttered. "Look, I have to update my appearance. I'm under contract." Now she was curt and short. "I just— There are things I have to do to survive." She turned abruptly, grabbing both of his hands in hers. "Just be careful when it comes to contracts. I know that makes no sense to you now and I really can't explain what I am talking about, but you will understand soon enough. Promise me you will not sign any contracts."

"I... I promise." Luca sounded unsure.

"Say it. Say it all." Quinn pleaded with him, which felt out of character for her, even to herself. "I need to know you will keep this promise. Promise me, please."

Luca looked at her incredulously. Clearly, none of this made any logical sense to him. Surely she appeared emotional, which he also didn't understand. But her insistence was enough for him to do whatever she asked.

"I promise I will not sign any contracts. I promise." Luca's tone reassured her as she regained her composure.

Quinn shook her head and pulled her hands back. "I'm sorry. That was out of line. You don't owe me anything."

"But I owe you everything. Because of you, I'm going to have a chance to live in the BioDome with my brother. He'll be safe. That's an amazing gift. I don't know if I can ever thank you enough."

LUCA'S GRATITUDE SEEMED to bounce right off Quinn. She lamented, "Don't thank me. You clearly don't understand what you're walking into but that's on purpose. No one really knows before they get there." Quinn stood up and took in a deep breath. "Let's get started. First, we need to work on your maneuvering. Those feet are a little slow." She swatted his arm as he looked down at his feet. "First rule. Always keep your chin up. You can't attack or defend if you're looking at the ground."

Luca looked up just in time to avoid Quinn's hand rushing toward his cheek, causing him to stumble backward.

"Hey!" he yelled, raising his arms defensively. "What the..." he said trying to catch his balance as she swung at him again with the other hand, forcing him to take another step back.

She stepped forward and swung yet another time.

This time, it was too much, and he couldn't stay balanced. Falling hard onto the ground,he was sure he broke his butt but instead of stopping, Quinn kept coming toward him. "What's going on? Why are you..." Luca tried as he crab-walked backward.

"Training," she grunted, still pushing forward. "The arena doesn't wait for you to be ready. Rule two. You must always be ready for an attack."

Luca's legs gave out under the pain. Dropping back to the ground, he raised his arms to shield his face.

"Stop, Quinn! Stop!"Luca shouted but she was now punching him as she overtook him. "Quinn!" He managed to grip one of her wrists and fought to get the other. "Quinn!"

The look in her eyes was fierce as she struggled against him. Something told Luca this was not about training. This was not about him or the arena. It was about the words he'd pulled from her, about how he made her feel something.

"I'm sorry, Quinn." He shifted his body around to give himself more leverage, pulling her into him instead of pushing her away. "Quinn,I'm sorry you have to deal with all this."

THE HOT TEARS HIT QUINN'S eyes and the harder she struggled, the less she could keep them at bay. Luca had her by the wrists and worse had pulled her into a strong embrace.She heard his apologies, but they didn't register as she started to cry uncontrollably. Luca held her until she went still, until she could breathe again. When she regained all her senses, she realized he was running his hand through her hair and had wrapped his arm around her waist. For a moment, she thought she should be repulsed, but this felt natural between them.

She cleared her throat and started to pull away. Luca released her at the first tug, obviously not wanting her to feel any more discomfort. As she stepped back, looking at him this way, he seemed charming and sweet. If only their circumstances were different. Maybe they could make a life together. Her body shivered as she shook off the events of this moment.

"Back to business." She sighed.

"What was that?" Luca insisted. "I think I have a right to know especially if we're going to be embroiled in combat like that."

"It was nothing,"Quinn said fiercely,preparing to attack him again.

"That wasn't nothing." Luca stood up and backed away. "You need to be honest with me and yourself.That wasn't nothing." He put his hands up defensively. "I don't know you well, but I know you need to talk about this."

"I don't need to talk about anything.We just need to work." Quinn said through gritted teeth.

"Sit down and talk to me!" He motioned to the bench. "Sit down!"

"Where was this confidence an hour ago?" Quinn looked shocked.

"You need to talk about this." Luca pressed. "There's not a whole lot I can say. It's not something I can openly discuss, Luca. You wouldn't understand."

"Why don't you let me try? Just tell me why you have to make all these changes. That's all we need to talk about." He sat down on the bench, patting the seat next to him and looking at her with a coy look on his face.

The desperation she saw in his eyes softened her, made her chuckle and she didn't see the harm in talking about her contract. Maybe it would relieve some of her stress and she did feel like she could trust him. Besides, who would he tell? He didn't know anyone inside the Dome yet and no one could know they were training. Technically they were cheating, and she already explained that to him.

"Fine." She huffed as she sat down next to him. "I have to update my appearance, but he has made some concessions. I get to choose."

"Is it painful?" Luca looked at her with concern written all over his face.

"Not sure. It might be if I didn't have such a high tolerance for pain. Did you not see all the scars? Did you not notice this side of my head?"

She ran her hand over the bald side and raised her eyebrows at him. "I have almost literally been brought back from death. I think I can handle a little scar removal."

"That doesn't really answer my question," Luca sucked in the corner of his mouth and narrowed his eyes at her. "Does it hurt?"

"Only a little bit and only the day after the procedures and for a few days after that." Quinn gave a weak smile. "A very small price to pay for my freedom."

"Pay for your freedom?" Luca's eyes went wide,and he tilted his head at her.

She slapped her hand over her mouth. That was a little too much information. How could she explain that without revealing everything she couldn't say?

"Look, I signed a contract for a sponsorship to get into the Dome. It's a possibility when you get to the later rounds. My sponsor kinda...owns me a little, until I work off the debt." Quinn fidgeted with her fingers as she looked down at her lap.

"How exactly do you have to work off your debt Quinn?" Luca's voice was barely above a whisper. She could almost see his brain working as all the pieces came together in his head. "Am I a part of working off that debt? Is all of this, pretending to be my friend while we train, working off your debt?"

"Yes and no." She answered him quietly as she shook her head. "I do things for him. Things out here. I recruit people for the arena. I scout the next set of contestants, so he can run his underground gambling ring. I thought I was close to working off the debt, but I forgot about a clause about room and board." She sat up straight, turning to look at him, gripping him by the shoulders. "It was the contact! He captured me with the contract! Which is why you can never sign one!"

"I already promised, didn't I?" Luca said. "But that's before you really understood. The consequences of the clauses. Fixing my scars..."

"I like your scars. They tell your story.Each story makes you who you are. Your scars don't make you look ugly. They show who you are to the world."Luca said, a stupid grin widened on his face the more he talked about it.

"Thanks. I think. It's just that... The only way to work off my debt is the alternative option. Otherwise, my debt will just keep mounting." Quinn refused to look up from her hands as she spoke.

"What is the alternative payment?" Luca set his hand on hers. "Quinn, do you have to do things you don't want to do? I mean, besides changing your appearance?"

Quinn looked up at him. The answer was written in her eyes, but she couldn't bring herself to say it to him. If she answered, he would know too much for this arrangement to work and if she didn't, this arrangement was bound to fall apart, and she would incur Pyrious' wrath.

Luca shot upward to his feet. "Never mind. You're right. It's none of my business. I don't want to know. Don't tell me." He began to pace and run his hands through his hair. "If you tell me, I'll feel like I need to do something about it and that will just complicate things. Let's get training. Come beat me up. Please, just come beat me up."

She shook her head. "No more beating. Just one more rule and this one you have to do based solely on trust because there is no way I can explain it. Do you trust me?" Quinn looked up expectantly.

Luca stopped pacing," Do I have any other choice?"

"Not really. If you don't follow the rules, our deal is off."

"Fine. I will trust you and not ask any questions about the last rule of the day," Luca relented.

"Okay. Since you have agreed to trust me..."

"Under duress," Luca murmured.

"Regardless. Do you agree to the terms of this agreement?" Quinn stood up.

Luca looked at her blankly." I thought you said not to enter into any contracts."

"This isn't a contract. It's an agreement between two civilized people who have the same amount of power over each other's lives." Quinn reasoned.

"No, you hold power over my life while I have no power over yours," Luca corrected.

"You have more power over me than you might think." Her eyes went wide as she slapped her hand over her mouth again. After a moment to recover, she looked at him hard. "So, do we have a deal?"

"Just tell me what the rule is already!" Luca exclaimed.

"This will be one of the hardest things you will ever do. You'll have to call off sick from work and you will have to keep Warren home from his studies until the withdrawal symptoms pass." Quinn began to explain.

"What are you talking about? Withdrawal symptoms? Missing work?" Luca looked at her incredulously.

"And you cannot tell the doctors or the Guard what you're doing." Quinn moved in and they were now almost nose to nose. "Do you understand the terms, Luca?"

He couldn't help but put his hands in hers even though he wanted to do more. "Just tell me what this is. Please give me the rule."

"Last rule for the day. No more meds. You can't take them, but you still need to get them like you are taking them. And I would stop giving them to your brother if I were you."

Luca pushed her back, studying her intently, probably hoping this was a cruel joke. She returned the seriousness to her face and hardened the look in her eyes. He opened his mouth but before he could formulate a thought, she put a finger to his lips.

"You agreed. No questions. No explanations. And you said you would follow the rule. I promise one day, this will all make sense, but it can't make sense today because I cannot explain." Quinn said.

"But...we'll die faster. I've seen what happens when people don't take them. I don't understand why you would want to hurt me like that." Luca said.

"I would not intentionally put you in harm's way. I promise. And I would never do anything to cause you pain unless it was absolutely necessary," Quinn said, trying to move closer.

"How can I know that? We barely know one another,"Luca said, stepping away from her advance.

"Because you're the only way I will ever get my freedom from...all the things you don't want to know about. You're my ticket out," Quinn said.

"So, you are using me." Luca sounded hurt and torn.

"Don't act so high and mighty. You're using me too!" Quinn replied defensively.

Luca turned, looking down at his hands.

Quinn said, "You know I'm right. We are using one another for our own personal gains. You need to remember this is an arrangement. Not a friendship. Not a relationship. A simple agreement to better our circumstances."

"You're right. We're both vested in this for personal reasons." Luca turned to face her. "Let's keep this from getting personal and recognize this is business, an agreement. I needed the reminder this was business and if it's necessary for me to stop taking the meds, that is what I will do even if I don't understand why."

Eleven

Luca decided he would quit the meds first to see what would happen. If there were adverse effects it would look like a virus, especially if he came down with something followed by his brother rather than both of them experiencing it at the same time. Within a few days, Luca was glad he formulated the plan prior to quitting the meds cold turkey. Quinn had insisted they put off training while he suffered from the after effects she called 'withdrawal.'

Luca couldn't eat, and his skin felt like it was on fire and like ants were crawling all over him simultaneously, not that he'd seen any ants in real life. But he'd watched plenty of historical nature vids showing ants and how they moved and worked in colonies. If he ate, he would throw up most of it, but he drank water as Quinn had instructed. But no matter how much he managed to keep down, cold sweat and restlessness coupled with a lack of any energy made worse by not being able to sleep kept him on edge and made him feel bad because he planned to put Warren through the same thing.

Late one night while posting his latest pics, he remembered a time when his mother had refused the medicine. Her symptoms were worse, and her body barely made it through. The doctors said it was the flu and it could end her, but it hadn't. He was amazed by how strong his mother actually was, holding on as long as she had. Luca thought she wanted Warren to be settled into a specialization, so she could leave Luca with less worries.

Dragging himself to his bed from the bathroom, Luca grabbed the empty bowl off his desk. He set it on the table next to the bed and hoped he would finally get some sleep. Suffering from mild hallucinations, he was certain he'd had complete conversations with many people, his dead father being one. Warren tried to convince Luca their father was dead, but he wouldn't hear it.

Now, in this brief moment of lucidity, he knew he hadn't talked to his father. Luca knew he had not visited the Dome and won some honorary award. He couldn't trust what he saw and read on his feed; thus he set himself up to avoid everyone until this passed.

On the calendar over the desk, Luca checked off another day. This was day four. Quinn said he would be better within a week or two. All he had to do was hold out for three more days. Pulling his covers over his head, he pulled his pillow over the other side of his head and laid on his side. Normally he could not sleep in this position but right now, it was the only comfortable position for Luca to lie down.

His eyes burst open, Luca sat straight up. Someone was in his room. Looking around, he saw someone in the chair at the desk.

"It's okay, Luca. It's me." said Quinn, rising. She sat down next to him on the bed. "I just wanted to check on you. I know the withdrawal can be difficult. Do you need anything?"

He just stared at her. She was wearing the hoodie from when they first met and none of her scars were healed but underneath the hoodie was the red dress from the night she snuck into his room.

"Maybe I can help you take a shower. That should help you feel better. More put together." She began to tug at his shirt to help him take it off, but he resisted. "It's okay. I've already seen everything anyway. Besides, the sooner you feel better, the faster we can get back to training. This is just a business arrangement."

"You're just trying to help," Luca muttered almost incoherently.

"Yes, I am simply here to help and I'm telling you, a shower will help you feel better. You're really sweaty and gross." Quinn made a face of disgust at him. "But you're really weak and I want to make sure you don't hurt yourself."

With that reasoning, he stopped resisting her and she helped him remove his shirt and get into the shower. When he got out of the shower, Quinn was gone. In his haze, Luca didn't give it a second thought. Back in his bed, he thought he heard someone again. Across the room, Quinn was in his drawer pulling out clothes for him to wear. Had she been there the whole time?

"You're pretty quiet and quick," Luca commented.

Quinn turned to face him, pants in hand. "Side effect of the arena and my current job."

As she tossed him clothes, he wriggled under the covers to put them on. Looking at the items, he realized she hadn't tossed him a shirt,but she had closed the door and now came toward him to sit on his bed again.

Quinn ran her hands through his wet hair, "I hope you feel a little better. I know you smell better." smiling at him, her eyes twinkled a little.

"I feel a little cold. Can you grab me a shirt?" he asked earnestly.

Quinn chuckled, "I can keep you warm. Body heat would be more effective." She motioned for him to slide over, crawling under the covers and pressing her body against his.

They had been close before and she had even been this closet to his face when they were training, but this was different. He couldn't find the right word to call it. All he could focus on was her warm body against his. Her body was against his. Realizing she had removed the dress and was only wearing the hoodie and whatever was underneath the dress forced a quick breath as his heart began to race again. How had he not noticed?

"Quinn," he cleared his throat, trying to sound casual. "Where's your dress?"

"I thought you might like it better this way." Quinn whispered in his ear.

Then she kissed his lobe gently, before moving her mouth across his cheek and meeting his lips with hers. She was gentle, which felt like an odd juxtaposition from her features, which made her look tough and hard. Her hand caressed one cheek as the other worked its way down his back.

Somehow, her hands felt softer than they usually did, no evidence of blisters, scars or tough skin. He breathed her scent in slowly, raising one hand to run through her hair until it came to rest gently on the nape of her neck. Closing his eyes, he felt her lips press over and over against his, every touch amplified by the feelings he had for her. She pulled back and looked him deep in the eyes. Her look was sweet, tender and soft.

"I...uh. Quinn. What..."

She placed a finger on his lips and shook her head then pushed him onto his back, climbing on top of him. Fingers running through his chest hair, she leaned down, kissing him again over and over. His hands found her hips and rested there until he felt comfortable going further.

Then Luca groped her ass, massaging it softly with his hands. He moved to her back, under the hoodie, inching fingers up her spine slowly as she writhed on top of him. She pushed herself back up, running her hands over his upper body, letting her fingers linger along his muscle lines as she smiled at him.

One hand rose up. Holding his breath, he watched as she started to slowly unzip the hoodie. He stopped her.

"Quinn, are you sure? I mean, this could mess with the business." Luca looked at her expectantly but kicked himself deep down. Why did he have to stop her or say anything at all? When would he ever get this chance again?

She moved his hand up, kissing his palm and then his wrist, finally placing it on her hip. Luca's eyes went wide as she continued to remove the jacket and toss it toward the desk. Luca followed it, realizing the door was open.

She leaned back against him, "It's okay. Warren's asleep. I checked. We'll be quick and quiet."

Sitting back up, she moved her hand slowly down his chest. "Luca." The way she said it made his whole body shiver in delight. "Luca."

He couldn't believe it. This was happening. Deep down, he couldn't convince himself this would be a bad thing and part of him knew he wanted this. Suddenly, the look on Quinn's face turned harsh. She slapped him.

"Luca!" she yelled."Luca!"

His eyes flew open in time to stop Warren in mid- swing to slap him again.

"Wake up! Luca!" Warren cried out.

Luca looked at Warren's hand under the weight of the heavy haze in his head. What was Warren doing in his room? Looking around, he saw no signs of Quinn or of him taking a shower even though he was soaked in sweat.

"You're awake! I thought you were dead until you started calling for someone named Quinn." Warren said. "Who's Quinn?"

Luca couldn't process the question. He just stared at Warren.

"Luca. Who is Quinn?" Warren persisted. Luca couldn't answer. "Whatever. Glad you're awake." Warren wrenched his wrist free and stepped back. "You need to clean your sheets and take a shower." He started to walk away. "The doc says your fever finally broke." Warren stopped in the doorway, gave Luca a strange look over his shoulder and left the room.

Twelve

Luca loved looking at his watch feed every evening now that his digital account was filling up with more Digicreds than he could have ever imagined using in his entire lifetime. People from all over his district were messaging him and requesting to follow his feed. The rush of opening the page and answering new messages, likes and follows made him happy in the moment, but he was beginning to slack off in his duties at the Burner and pulling back on training. He even forgot to help Warren study for his specialization testing. The only thing he cared about or for was the next time he could check his feed.He raced home, not to check on his mother or talk to Warren, but to open the feed and post something new.

Quinn's formula for posting was working so well, he couldn't have imagined something this simple would get him noticed. She did all the work for the posts, and he just had to upload them. After his latest post, he breathed a heavy sigh, scrolling through the feed for new comments.

Sometimes, he even went through other people's feeds, liking a few things but scouring the web for ideas and options. On occasion, he found himself scrolling through a Govpage he didn't like. If it didn't please him, he commented on how they could improve or messaged the owner to try harder.

Two weeks of obsession and all he had to show for it was a form of fame. People in his block were recognizing him and asking questions. He pictured himself as one of the stars of the 21st century, standing for photos and signing autographs. There was a world like that today, but it was inside the arena. Every person recognizing him from his feed was one step toward the arena games and a life of luxury inside the Dome.

From out of nowhere, Quinn walked over and slapped his arm. The feed disappeared as he glowered at her.

"What the hell, Quinn?" he shouted.

"I could say the same thing, lazy arena boy." Quinn's tone laced with disdain. "How's the withdrawal?"

"Gone." Luca said surprised. "Not feeling any withdrawal symptoms. In fact, I've never felt better."

"Interesting." Quinn grimaced."Sounds like you're trading one addiction for another."

Luca raised an eyebrow. "What do you mean?"

"What do you mean what do I mean?" Quinn squared to him, clearly preparing for training.

Luca automatically started running through his arena warm up drills. "Trading one addiction for another. I didn't know the meds were addictive." He replied, standing more out of an automatic response to her stance than using actual thought processes.

"Any medicine is addictive because you are putting foreign chemicals in your body, some not meant for human consumption. This causes a response your body would not normally have or forces a response your body cannot do naturally because of some other deficiency and after enough time, you've conditioned your body to rely on the meds." Quinn explained, stepping back and watching him go through the motions of warm-up.

"Those meds were designed to be addictive. But really, anything can become an addiction."

"What do you mean by anything?" Luca jabbed and stretched and danced as they had done every training session.

The movements had a rhythm and timing he had become accustomed to, and it felt good to be in a routine he knew. So much lately was new and unfamiliar.

"Take this warm-up for instance. You could almost say you're so used to doing the same thing, you're addicted. You need to do it to feel good. As long as the response is the same, your body has become accustomed to every movement." Quinn explained. "It can be like that with the stream and the feed. You're becoming addicted to your own popularity, but it only makes you feel good as long as you can look at it or see your likes and follows go up. So much so, you think you are the authority on all things in the feed, thinking you can discourage others or make fun of the fact they are not as popular as you." The corners of her mouth turned up as she side-stepped.

Luca spun and nearly lost his balance. "See, you are coming out of your trance-like warm-up state just because I did something different."

He stepped back, to process what she said, knowing his face showed his feelings—of incredulous disapproval. "I am not addicted to my feed. I am not so selfish as to only think about the stream and my feed."

"Really, when was the last time you talked to your mom or spent time with Warren since your feed started to take off?" Quinn folded her arms, giving him a look he interpreted as 'Miss Know-It-All' in previous conversations.

"I don't know. I'm so busy right now..." Luca stopped and thought hard to give a concrete answer to the question but couldn't find a satisfactory answer to prove her wrong.

"It's okay. It kinda happens to everybody in the beginning. Most don't come out of it though because no one is watching out for them. Just prepare yourself for the adrenaline rush of the Arena itself. That is super addictive. You need to fightthat natural urge,and you can start now." She stepped closer to him. "New rule. You can only post at night, but you cannot look at your feed, the stream or your messages except on Sunday nights. And no more looking at other people's pages." She put her hands on her hips. "I am tired of intercepting your awful messages. Doing things like that will destroy everything we have managed to build regarding your image."

"I am being helpful. Those people need to know." Luca replied indignantly.

"You're being rude, and the troll-like behavior will not be tolerated any longer. No more comments on other people's feeds. I don't have the time to watch your every comment all the time."

The light went on in Luca's head, "You can intercept my comments?"

"We can watch everything you do on the stream.

And we are, or at least we're trying to because we are doing everything to ensure you don't screw this up." She stepped closer, putting her hands on his shoulders. "You need to appear to be a nice guy. Someone who is almost too nice. And you're also considered old for the competition. They won't consider extending you an invite if you ruin your reputation trying to, what did you call it...help people."

"Wait, I thought the invite was automatic once you hit a certain level of follows and likes." Luca said, looking at her quizzically.

"That's what they want you to think but it's not. Only people in the Dome know it's not because they need to keep the general masses occupied with hope, even if it is a false hope and the game is rigged." Quinn replied avoiding his gaze as her hands slipped off his shoulders.

It's just business, Luca thought taking in a deep breath. It really is all just business. "What is the invite based on then?" he asked.

She took a swing at him. He dodged it reflexively, deflecting it with his hand and responding with a cross punch. Quinn deflected and responded by trying to hit him again. This all felt like slow-motion to him as he decided not to deflect but grab her wrist.

"What is the invite based on, Quinn?"

"A lot of factors. The producers have a whole list." Quinn said, yanking her wrist free in one movement.

Luca took the opportunity to practice her move, mimicking every inch of it to learn her skills. She countered easily and he noted how.

"What's a producer?" he said as he repeated her motions over and over again.

"They're the panel of people who are responsible for all content on the stream." Quinn answered, correcting some of his motions without interfering too much with his practice or rhythm.

"So, they pick the contestants." Luca said. "And what are they looking at when they choose? Are there guidelines?"

"More like a list of factors," she said as she moved in to teach him an extension from the move he was perfecting, allowing him to continue the motion from defense to attack.

"What are the factors?" he asked, adjusting to the new move and practicing it to make the two techniques appear seamless. Quinn made that easy as she adapted her actions and reactions to what he was doing or needed to do next.

"Well, age is a big one and I've already told you you're kinda old for the arena." Quinn smiled, still correcting his motions.

"Okay, what other factors are counting against me?" Luca asked.

"Popularity. No matter how hard you try, people can see you're old. But this plays well into the entertainment factor they consider. You have gotten into a little trouble making yourself popular, so you have a bit of a selling point. You've got a great back story and motivation. A younger player doesn't yet know how to break the rules like you do. But there's more to it."

"Is that why you had me change all that stuff on my feed, to give me more entertainment value?"

"As you are aware, the arena is for entertainment. If you don't have any entertainment value, then you won't make it in." Quinn continued. "Skill and specialization may work against you. Some people specialize in the investigative arts because they learn how to fight and deflect, which are useful skills in the arena."

Luca stopped moving. "Oh, I never thought of that." He stood there without returning to his previous activity. "So, do I have anything going for me really? I mean, factor- wise?"

"Well, like I said, you have a great motivation that really pulls at people's heartstrings." Like maneuvering a puppet, Quinn moved him back into a defensive position, but he didn't hold it. "And you have the gamblification number in the right range?"

"What in the world is gamblification?" Luca shook his head.

"It's the science and math of who makes a good character to bet on and who stands to make the panel the most money. As an older contestant, you go in the underdog category with long odds. People tend to bet on an underdog but only if they think he has a chance to win. According to your feed, you're super-nice and you do things that don't put you in danger or get you in trouble to raise your numbers. That means you're less likely to be ruthless in the arena, according to gamblification. When you win, less people will have bet on you in the first round, and they won't have to pay out as many long shots as well as not having to pay off the bigger betters on contestants with higher odds of winning. It's all very technical. Your gamblification number right now almost guarantees you an invite to the first round. It's only a matter of time considering the other positive factors you have going for you."

Luca motioned at her, "So gamblification number, the fact I'm not ruthless and my back-story are all I have going for me." He shook his head as it dropped to look at the floor, pacing with his hands on his hips. "Wait! You said there were some other factors in my favor."

"Well..." she huffed in shock. "Like you don't know."

His pacing ceased.Turning on his heel to look at her seriously, "Don't know what?"

Slapping him on the shoulder, "Oh come on. You know. Don't make me say it." He just looked at her. He had no idea what she meant. "You're. Well,"releasing an exasperated sigh. "You're very good-looking okay. Handsome. Downright sexy."

Luca was dumbfounded. "I'm sexy?" His eyes rolled upward as he tried to process the statement, especially coming from Quinn. "I've never really considered myself to be handsome and there's never really been anyone... I mean, when it comes to love and stuff..." he stammered, stopping before he said something to make a complete ass of himself.

He looked at Quinn in complete disbelief, but as he looked, he had an epiphany. As her scars had disappeared and her skin became less blotchy, he could see how she could make it on her looks alone. In fact, he mused to himself that her having to fight with a holographic avatar only did her a disservice as her looks would make anyone think twice about striking her with the way she looked now. He couldn't imagine how awe inspiring she must have been back then, especially if you considered she was a nice person.

"Well, apparently confidence is not a strong factor. Your profile would indicate otherwise but apparently, you are not aware or confident." Quinn bit her lip. "Look, it's going to be an issue. I can guarantee, with your looks, they're going to pair you up with a 'love interest' for the partner exhibition matches."

"What do you mean?" Luca asked concerned. "Okay, normally, the exhibitions are for showing off your gear and technique or for creating a following but that's why they usually pair males with males and females with females as they are in two different categories in the arena." Quinn paused, grabbing Luca's hand and leading him back to the bench. "With your looks, they'll pair you up with a female. It's the only time you'll fight with or against females in the arena.While the matches don't mean anything, they use them to set the odds based on performance. They also use couples to set up entertainment stories."

"Those were manufactured? I thought everyone picked who they fought with." Luca said as he sat down.

Quinn sat next to him, "How can they choose a perfect stranger from another district clear across the country to be their partner on the basis they are in love with them?" she reasoned, and he saw her point.

"I guess I should have been looking closer. The content is misleading." Luca rubbed his hands nervously.

"It's all produced for entertainment and to make money, whichever serves their needs. The couples are entertainment, made up to create tension and hope. If you can find love in the arena and you both manage to make it to the Dome. Can you imagine the story and hope it would create?" Quinn said, clearly hoping he was understanding what she was talking about.

"And you think they'll put me into one of these couples?" Luca was completely terrified.

"Yes, and they'll expect you to be somewhat of a romantic-type person. Saying and doing affectionate things." Quinn said. "Do you know how to do that stuff? If you're not convincing, they'll find a way to toss you out of the competition."

"I... uh...I'm," sweat ran down his forehead and cheeks like he had never experienced. The pressure was too much. "I'm not very experienced. I've only really had one girlfriend, and I think she would tell you I did not chase her down or have to woo her. It was a long time ago too. I was only 14, I think."

Quinn's cheeks puffed up with air, releasing it all loudly before continuing, "So, not so confident in the romance area. I guess we will have to practice that too. I can give you pointers and honestly, we'll have to practice some things that will make us both uncomfortable. But it's like you've said before, this is just a business arrangement, right?"

Luca flashed to his wild dream. He had forgotten how awkward their few training nights had been after he recovered from the hallucinations and dreams of withdrawal. Looking at Quinn made him feel different now. More and more, he was realizing what he dreamed about might be his actual desire, but he couldn't get involved with her. To distract from that, he'd researched contracts and knew now that breaking a contract would cause them both to be put to death. Besides, he doubted she was really interested in him despite the fact she said he was sexy.

"Right. Just business." he replied, trying to convince himself it was the withdrawal forcing those thoughts in his head, but his confidence wavered.

"You're going to need to say that with more confidence. Like you believe it without any doubts. Consider it practice for the arena drama." Quinn shook her head.

Luca looked at her and swallowed hard, eyes wide. "It is just business," he mustered without much confidence.

"I can see this is going to take a lot of work.

Hopefully you take to it like you did the fighting. If so, you'll learn it all quickly and we'll be able to move on."

Thirteen

Even though the house was enormous, Quinn felt cramped in the space. It was a five-story building with sprawling rooms, ornate columns, gold-leaf ceilings and meticulously marbled and hardwood floors. The fourteen- foot ceilings were more than twice her height by comparison, causing every sound to echo in any room making it impossible to sneak in or out of anywhere. Also, for Quinn, this would always feel like a prison despite its lavish furnishings and finishes. It was also one of the few homes used for public functions and it acted as part of the Dome structure, as the garage had two exits, one outside and one inside as well as a subfloor with passages no one really knew about. Pyrious' great, great, great something-or-other had owned the land where the original Dome was built and that allowed the family access with some liberties.

She sat down at the vanity, wishing she could call Nallie to work her magic. But seeing her reflection in the mirror told her she no longer needed Nallie. Her new, or as Pyrious referred to it "restored," appearance was a blessing and a curse. More people noticed her now when they went out; however, she no longer had to suffer Pyrious' exhibition-like behavior with Nallie. She wasn't sure which she preferred more, the lack of excuse her acquiescence gave Pyrious to intrude like he did or extended conversations with someone who seemed to embrace the Dome lifestyle of carefree fun and extended boredom. Especially those who now wanted her to alleviate their tedium. If one made it past the age of forty, which was the standard in the Dome, she imagined the same things would become tiresome and boring. One person could literally "see it all" before they were even close to death. That accounted for the rising drama and persistence of violence in the arena. The producers were having to go to further lengths to keep the Dome entertained. The masses didn't matter.

She picked up the dress Halstead had laid out for her and headed to the bathroom.This was the only place she could voluntarily lock herself in, which gave her a safe haven from Pyrious' prying eyes. This dress was not as figure fitting as the red one and the heels were not as high but something for the competitors' welcome banquet would not be suited when attending the arena to scout for new sportsman. She should be grateful for any concession to the actual work she had to do.

Braiding her hair delicately proved to be a little more difficult after the training session with Luca. They had been working on hand releases. Her right hand had been hit, swatted and wrenched more than she would have liked, making it sore and tired. Her fingers struggled to hold the hair in place securely enough to anchor the intricate braid. After a dozen tries, it finally held. She added small clips with silk flowers to her hair as a finishing touch. Finally, she looked ready to grace the masses. Now more than ever, she wished she could wear a mask.

Pyrious stormed through her door without knocking, growling in frustration when he saw the bathroom door closed. Wiggling the handle, he grunted again when he found it locked.

"Get out here, girl. I have a present for you," he shouted as he pounded relentlessly on the door.

Quinn frowned and rolled her eyes as she reached for the knob. Pulling her shoulders back, she tried to look and feel confident. As she swung the door open, Pyrious almost fell to the floor having leaned in to knock so hard.

Catching himself, she saw a tall stack of papers in his hand. "The new contract?" Quinn asked, holding out a hand for it.

"Two copies of it. Both to be signed right away," he winked at her as he pulled a pen from his pocket with his free hand.

"Not before I read every word," she pulled the papers out of his hand. "In case you're trying to trick me somehow."

"Oh, by all means, have your lawyer take a look at them," he mused as his grin spread from ear to ear and laughing at his own joke.

"I'm smart enough to understand it myself. I understood the firstone. Remember?" Quinn quipped.

Pyrious huffed, "I suppose you did with all your negotiations and all the draftsat my expense." He folded his arms like a pouting toddler.

"You still managed to get what you wanted,"she replied feigning a sincere smile.

"Until now," he forced her to take the pen. "Unless you just sign them."

"No way. I have more bargaining power now than I did then," she said. "I'm also older and wiser."

"I imagine neither will work in my favor," Pyrious whined. "Why not just get it over with? Then we could, you know, get the first awkward time over with." Now his grin showed every tooth as he smacked her across her backside.

Quinn heeled around, moving in quickly to place the pen on his throat just above his Adam's apple. "I'd be careful how you handle yourself before I sign this contract." She pressed the sharp tip of the pen into his throat hard, but not hard enough to break skin.

Pyrious grabbed her hips, pulling her in closer. Ripping her body out of his grasp, she threw the pen across the room, hard enough it lodged into the wall by the desk. Following it, she placed the contracts on the desk and turned to face Pyrious again.

"Next time, I won't be so nice," she said.

"Neither will I," he chuckled, putting his hand on his hip and motioning for her to take him arm. "The arena awaits." She grabbed her bag and walked toward him. "You're not planning to try an escape, are you?"

Pyrious joked, laughing at his cruelty so hard it took every ounce of Quinn's control not to knock out all his teeth.

She took his arm, seething silently, "No, I have a training session right after the last round. It would be difficult to train in this thing."

Pyrious stopped, "So, there's little chance you'll get to that contract before morning I imagine." He was whining a little again.

"I thought I was here to help you make money. Would you like me to neglect your latest cash cow?" He looked down at her disapprovingly. "To miss a session might mean he will drop in authentic likes and follows. We're very close to getting an invite. I know it will come any day now."

"It better," Pyrious huffed, escorting her out of the room.

Quinn always found the opening ceremonies of a new round so boring. Looking around the arena, this one was modeled after ancient Roman architecture, specifically the Coliseum although she imagined the original was much larger and had dirt for floors. It was the only building allowed to have an individual BioDome over it and that guaranteed it would maintain itself well beyond its years.

Today, they were in the Northwest Coalition, and the new crop of contestants did not appear to have enormously redeeming qualities. This was the district with the least amount of likes,follows and feed activity. Quinn attributed it to the laid-back attitude of the people here. No one really cared to be involved; therefore, it was easier to get into the arena in this district than any other. But few of them made it past the regional rounds.

Each contestant was paraded out. Their best feed hits playing on the screens around them. Then they showed off their avatar and the armaments they had managed to purchase as the announcer gave a short bio over the sound system.

Finally, they were subjected to two minutes of pandering to the audience, and the contestant was led to a seat on one side of the arena or the other based on biological sex.

When all the contestants were marched through,then the random partners would be chosen. Quinn knew there was nothing random about it. These partner matches were chosen long before any contestant set foot in the arena.

Then they would watch the ten-minute partner matches designed to show off each of the contestants' combat skills.

By the third parading contestant, Quinn was ready to go. She looked at Pyrious who eyed her suspiciously.

Shaking his head at her, "If I allow you to go now, will you get to the contract before dawn?"

"Of course," she lied.

"Then go train arena boy."

She started to rise but he slammed his hand down on her knee forcing her to hit the seat hard, "But if he doesn't get an invite by the end of next week, I imagine I would think you've broken all contracts and betrayed me." His tone was harsh.

Quinn swallowed hard, "I told you. He is so close. It should only be a few more days. I know we have the attention of the producers."

"I hope you're right, for your sake," Pyrious' grimaced at her. "And his." He released his grip and she removed her heels to start up the stairs making good time in bare feet.

Changing in the car proved more difficult than she anticipated. She knew the driver reported everything and would not be surprised if there was a secret private feed somewhere in this car for Pyrious to watch everything happening inside, whether for the first time or for review.

She shivered at the thought and settled for putting on her pants and boots under the skirt. The dress would have to wait until they arrived at the warehouse. Once inside, she would find a hidden corner and finish changing there.

Despite having left the arena early, she assumed Luca would beat her to the meet-up spot. He always managed to get there first, and Quinn wasn't sure what his secret was.

She raced into the warehouse, but Luca was nowhere in sight. Breathing a sigh of relief, she managed to find a cozy and private place to finish changing. Then she hit the middle of the floor to stretch and warm up. After thirty full minutes of warming up alone, Quinn stood up and looked around.

"Luca?" she called out. "Luca, this is not a funny joke."

She jogged around the floor, checking every hiding spot she could find, even if she knew he would never fit in it. Still no sign of him. Moving up floor by floor and searching each thoroughly still produced no sign of him. Hands on her hips, she did a final scan of the top floor before repeating the process back down to the first.

By the time she returned to the first floor, it was a full hour after their scheduled meeting time. Did she give him directions to the wrong place? No. She was certain she picked here because it was the closest location to the Northwest Coalition's arena. Was this the wrong day? No, it was opening ceremonies for the Northwest Coalition, and they could only practice when she was in the area. Where was Luca?

Quinn worked hard to mentally prepare for this training. They were supposed to work on his acting skills, to practice for the fake relationship she knew he would end up playing out to the audience in the arena. If the invite came too soon, he may not be ready. After waiting another hour, she returned to the car parked two buildings away in a decrepit parking garage. The car needed to stay out of sight of the guard while it waited for her as it was now after curfew.

She slammed into the back seat, dejected. Quinn had come to enjoy Luca's company. He was smart and witty and strong, not at all what she imagined when they made the proposal to Pyrious. Their growing closeness felt like more than friends. They were taking on the world together, one training session at a time. Having someone to face the world with was nice.Something deep down told her it was more than that though.

"That was short," the driver snapped.

"Yeah well," she sighed, leaning back and folding her arms. "He just wasn't that into me, I mean training tonight. If his head's not in it, I don't want to waste my time."

She huffed, pretending to be annoyed, not wanting to risk Pyrious finding out about Luca's no show, especially after the confrontation in the arena just hours earlier.

"Well, I suppose you have a point," the driver smiled in the rear-view mirror and started the car.

"Guess I am going to manage to read that contract tonight," she mumbled as the car roared out of the parking garage and up the disheveled pavement.

Fourteen

For the fourth session in a row, Quinn waited at their usual training spot. Unlike the first time Luca did not show up. She worked out for herself while waiting, never returning early. As the time ticked by today, she found herself anxious and worried. If she lost the golden goose, Pyrious would have her head on a platter, made worse by the fact she hadn't signed his contract yet. She wanted Luca to look it over. When she read it, she didn't see anything beyond what she discussed but Pyrious was sneaky. This was not his first negotiation and her first obviously hadn't gone well. She knew Warren was acclimated to law and mathematics because Luca mentioned it and wondered what type of specialization he could have with those two skills. They seemed contradictory until Quinn mentioned a few options, subduing his fears.

If Warren was acclimated to law and Luca was as intelligent as she thought and they studied Warren's work together; he might be able to help her understand everything and see if there were any loopholes in either contract. She had brought both to the last three training sessions, but Luca was still a no show and there was no indication as to why. Eyeing her bag and thinking of the papers inside, she swept it up and walked out of the old gym. Taking surface streets would be too dangerous in the afternoon but sneaking in through his window with the sun out would be equally so. She decided to approach via his front door.

Knocking rapidly, she put her ear up to the door to hear inside. Quick, light footsteps came toward her. It swung open to a young boy with dark hair and brown eyes. His feet were bare, and he looked no older than ten.

"Hello," Quinn said with a smile.

The boy's mouth gaped as he looked her up and down. She'd forgotten what a sight she could be.

"Is Luca home?" she knelt to meet him eye to eye. "What do you want to know about? Is it something about how I look?" He nodded and pointed to her head. Reflexively, she ran her hand over the scars. "Oh, those are just battle wounds."

"Are you a soldier?" the boy finally asked. "No, not really. I'm a friend of Luca's. From the Burner," she replied. "My name is Quinn." She held out her hand for him to shake it.

A grin spread across his face and his eyes began to twinkle. "Quinn huh?" he tried to shake her hand firmly, but it was smaller than she thought it would be. "I'm Warren."

"I figured." Quinn smiled. "You've got a pretty good grip there."

"So, Luca talks about me. I'm not surprised. Things like that happen when you're as awesome as me." Warren's smile grew wider and now she could count all his teeth.

"Apparently, Luca has mentioned me as well," she probed carefully, hoping he would invite her in.

"Well, kinda." Warren blushed. "Only once and... It was while he was sick." Warren explained, releasing her hand and stepping out of the way so she could come through the threshold.

"When he was sick huh?" Quinn gave him a quizzical look.

"It was kinda awkward," the blush spread to Warren's ears.

She ruffled his hair hoping it would make him more comfortable. "So, is Luca here?"

"He's in his room. Down the hall and to the right." Warren walked her to the hallway and motioned. "I hope he talks to you. Maybe you can get him to come out of there."

"Is he sick again?" Quinn asked. "Have you been sick? Is he able to afford your meds?" She wanted to have a better idea of what she was walking into.

"I never caught his virus, but I am down to a quarter pill because he hasn't worked for over a week, again." Warren's face turned sad. "I guess that couldn't be helped. You can talk to him about it, right? You know how to get him out of there?"

"Definitely." She smiled at him. "I'll see what I can do." She ruffled his hair again before marching down the hall.

The door was open. Luca was curled up on his bed. She swung the door shut. As it clicked into place, Luca rolled over.

"Warren, not now," he mumbled.

She plopped down on the foot of the bed. "Warren..." he struggled to maneuver under the

blanket because all the give was gone.

"A little over two months and this is what it comes to?" she seethed."You just don't want to bother anymore?"

"Quinn," Luca bolted upright. "What are you doing here?"

"Well, you haven't shown up to train all week," she punched the bed as her aggression boiled over. "Do you have any idea what position you have put me in? If Pyrious finds out you've pulled out of the deal, he'll take it out on me," she whispered tersely, leaning in. "Not to mention all the time I have wasted on you!" She stood up, pacing. "I've covered for you as long as I can and now I have to figure out what to tell Pyrious. I'll be lucky if he doesn't feed me to the dogs."

"What do you mean, Quinn? I don't understand..." Luca started.

"Of course, you don't understand. You have no idea what kind of dangerous world I live in. What the consequences for me would be. So selfish."

"Why? What? Selfish?" Luca wasn't quite following her words.

He threw the blanket off, approaching her. Grabbing her by the shoulders, he forced her to stop pacing. "What are you talking about?"

"If you wanted out, you needed to tell me. Just not showing up...that's just...I can't..." Quinn tried to resist but the tears came hot and fast as she started to cry, falling into his arms. "He just might kill me for this or worse."

"Worse?" Luca tried to steady her as he moved them both toward the foot of the bed.

"There are some things worse than death," she swallowed hard and sniffled.

"I'm not backing out of our deal," Luca said, smoothing her hair.

"What? Then why?" She looked up at him, wiping the wetness from her eyes with the back of her hand.

"My mom died, Quinn. She's dead,"he brushed her cheek lightly with his fingers. "I've been, a little. Well, I dunno."

"You're not backing out on the deal?" she swallowed hard trying to process. She sat up straighter. "Your mom's dead? I'm so sorry. I just thought...I don't know what I thought."

"It's okay, Quinn. I just haven't felt like going out," he said. "I needed to be here for Warren and well...it's just hard."

"You can't be here for Warren if you're not bothering to actually be here for him," Quinn reasoned. "He needs you to be with him."

"I guess I'm having trouble finding a reason to just do some things. I guess," his grin seemed forced.

"Well, at least I got you out of bed I guess," Quinn chuckled. "Maybe I can convince you to get dressed."

"I think Warren would like that,"Luca said.

"One step at a time. That's how you get through it. One moment at a time," Quinn said, rising to her feet and holding out her hands to get him to stand up.

"Where did you learn that?" Luca asked accepting her offer.

"I've had some bad times myself," she sucked in the corners of her mouth. "Luckily, I had someone to help me and now I'll be here to help you. The first step is to step forward."

He rose and stepped into her personal space, wrapping his arms around her. For a moment, she laid her head on his chest while he stroked her hair.

"That was pretty smooth. Maybe you don't need lessons," she looked up at him.

He placed his finger under her chin, lowering himself toward her. "It's easy when I'm with you."

She closed her eyes as he pressed his lips to hers. They tasted sweet. Placing her hands on the nape of his neck, she embraced him and held him close. He slid his hands down to her hips, pressing his hands into the small of her back. Too soon he tried to pull away. She wouldn't allow it and pressed her lips onto his over and over until he stepped back.

LUCA IMMERSED HIMSELF in touching her, running his hands up and down her back and over her ass. She ran her hands through his hair and down his chest, where they stopped and pushed him back. Taking in a deep breath, she pulled out of his embrace and stood up. Luca reached out, grabbing her hand, desperate for more but she wouldn't come close again.

Fifteen

"I cannot believe you would even consider signing this agreement, Quinn. You realize what he's asking you to do." Luca's look expressed his disgust. "To him or let him do to you?"

"Of course, I do Luca. But this is the only way I will ever gain my freedom," she sat down, fidgeting her fingers. "Besides, the contract is just a courtesy. He'll eventually take what he wants anyway."

"Eventually. You mean...he hasn't enforced the clause at all?" Luca sounded hopeful.

"What difference does it make? You don't understand, Luca.Eventually he will get his way," her voice sounded forlorn.

"Did you know?" Luca looked at her desperately. "When you signed the first contract? Did you know it would come to this?"

"Honestly," she fought back tears. "I didn't even bother to read it." She turned and took his hands in hers, "When I made it to the final rounds in the arena, I didn't have the Creds to survive. I'd spent most of them making my family as comfortable as possible as I couldn't choose who to take with me. I paid for my father to get an elevated position and for my brother and sister to specialize." She stared at their hands and shook her head, "I was desperate. And after so many years, someone like you coming along was just a fantasy."

"I'm not perfect and if I'm helping you break a contract, we could both hang," Luca mumbled. "I'd be willing to hang for you."

Quinn looked up at him, her eyes brighter than he'd seen them in a long time. "You mean, you would risk it...for me?"

Luca flushed until even his ears were bright red, "I'd do just about anything for you." He gave her a half-smile. "I mean, you're not like anyone I have ever met."

"You're definitely different than most people," Quinn was starting to grin. "But this contract is something I still have to do. I have to be with someone else."

"Why don't you just run away? You know your way around better than anyone." Luca teemed with excitement at the possibility. "We could run away together."

"Could you really leave Warren behind?" Quinn said. "I mean, I wouldn't want to force him to live a life of our choosing. And honestly, he deserves to make the choice."

She could tell her words took him back down to sullen. Leaving Warren would be difficult, and it would be like he was choosing Quinn over Warren, which is probably something he never wanted to do in the first place. His face echoed how he felt torn.

Luca stammered, "I..I... guess we could ask him." Quinn looked at him seriously and shook her head slowly, "I can't." If she shared this with him, she'd take yet another piece of his innocence. With a sigh, she tilted her chin upward and pointed.

with two fingers. "See the scar?" Luca leaned in closer. "It's a chip, like they used to do for dogs and cats. You know, pets, before the revolution. If I run off, they can turn it on and track me."

LUCA TOUCHED QUINN'S chin scar, breathing in deep. She smelled so nice. "Or, if they want," she gulped hard. "They can use it to shock me and kill me."

Luca pulled back a bit as she dropped her chin. They were almost nose to nose. He knew his eyes were full of shock and dread, he swallowed hard. They hadn't been this close physically since the other day and Quinn had made it plain something like that could never happen again. She halted the whole thing.

"You would really hang for me," her hand trembled as it moved down to his chest, feeling how fast his heart was beating.

"I'd do anything for you," the words choked out. He found his mouth unusually dry. "All you need to do is ask."

"Anything?" she whispered. "Anything at all?"

"Anything." he breathed her in. She smelled sweeter now and all he wanted was to taste her lips again.

"Then kiss me like..."

Luca leaned in and kissed her at the first hint of permission. She wanted it. This excited him.

QUINN FOUND KISSING Luca exhilarating and during these moments, she felt truly free. No one ruled over her. There were no contracts, no responsibilities, no constraints. Losing herself in this moment, she could easily forget the consequences of running away, as she would do so without doubt if Luca was with her.

He pulled away from her. "The contract appears to be on the up and up," he refused to meet her gaze. "I would do anything for you, Quinn. Well, almost, I guess." He felt her question before she could even ask it. "I can't share you, Quinn.I just can't stand the thought of sharing you." He paused, anger rising into his chest. "Especially with him."

He punched the stack of papers. The veins in his forehead pulsed and now he was white with anger.

"You wouldn't be sharing me," Quinn replied, trying to pull him in close again.

"You're right. He'll get to do it. Be with you," Luca pulled away and turned his back on her. "He gets to be with you, in that way," he motioned toward the contract. "While I just get to watch and want you from afar."

She walked up behind him, sliding her hands up his back and onto his shoulders. His shivers betrayed that her touch thrilled him. But he continued to ignore her. Her hands slid down over his chest, and she pulled him back into a strong embrace, resting her head on his back.

"You're not far away," she said, holding him tightly.

His hands raised to take hers, pulling them of his chest, pushing her back. He turned to face her. "You know what I mean."

"He gets to use my body. That's all." She looked at him in desperation, hoping he would understand. "You would be with me. In my heart." She put his hand on her sternum for him to feel how fast it was beating. "Knowing you and I are in this together might be the only way I get through the contract in one piece."

"But, Quinn, he will get to do those things to you. How can you separate that?" Luca was fighting to believe her.

"I'll be able to separate it," she bit her lip and continued timidly. "If you agree to be my first. Then he can't take the most important thing from me. He can't take away my choice in how I feel about you or the time we spend together. He would have no control over that."

"That's not exactly how this works," Luca said. "He still has all the control. You only choose to see he doesn't."

"Can't we make it work that way?" Quinn asked. "Are you trying to set me up? Was this always the plan? For me to allow you to sign that contract and then making me help you break it? Seriously, there are easier ways to kill yourself."

"Do you really think so little of me? I thought we had something between us. Something real." Quinn pushed back the pain of Luca's statements. "How could you think I WANT to sign this contract? If I had ANY choice in the matter, I would run. But I can't. I may not be signing the contract while someone holds a gun to my head, but you know as well as I do Pyrious already put it in the original contract, and he will take my soul if I don't give my body to him willingly. But it's only my body. You will protect my heart and soul." Stepping closer to him, he opened his arms to embrace her. "Please, Luca. Don't pull away now."

"I just don't know if I can share you like that. Just the thought of it makes me want his blood." Luca kissed the top of her head. "It's not right. Not like this."

"What's not right?" Quinn asked softly.

"The way you want this to happen. It's too forced," shaking his head but unwilling to let her go. "You're clearly not ready and it won't be right unless you are. Unlike Pyrious, that matters to me." He pushed her back but held her by the shoulders to look her in the eye. "Try to stall on signing the contract until you feel ready. Until something like that happens more naturally. I don't want to rush it, and I don't want you to regret it."

"I suppose that's fair," she whispered. "It's not like we're not going to have unlimited amounts of private time. At least, after you get your invite."

"Oh, that's right. I forgot to tell you. It came yesterday," he paused. She hasn't been able to hide her feelings as her look changed from tenderness to anger. "Before I read the contract. After I read it, I was so angry, I could only see red."

He relinquished his grip on her to walk over and shove the papers into her training bag, hiding them beneath some gear.

"Stall him as long as you can. I'll wait but I can't guarantee I won't hit him when I finally make it to the Dome."

"You'll have to learn some control. We are special attendees at almost all arena events. We go everywhere and anywhere." Quinn gave him a weak grin as Luca sat down in a huff.

"Then I really have to decide how much of this I can really take. I guess, stall him until we're both ready."

Sixteen

The car door opened. Quinn stepped out gingerly, looking at the arena. This one was modeled after arenasfor modern twenty-first century sports. Others hinted it was actually an original construction from that time, but she doubted it considering how much the upkeep would have cost. An entire floor of windows made her wonder if the arena was lit by the sun. Inside,she found herself in a long concrete hallway marked 'Concourse.' Vendors were strewn about along the corridor. The structure appeared to go in a circle with stairs and elevators to the upper floors at even intervals. How could someone find their way around some place so large? And you literally could walk in circles. Unless you noted the faces of a specific group of vendors, how would you know whether you had passed them before? Although the architecture was relatively plain, she marveled at the sheer scale of this arena. She hadn't been to this one previously.

Pyrious pulled her toward him and leaned into her ear, "The only reason you would ever find me this far into the outreaches is for your arena boy." He stroked her cheek as she pulled away. "Let's hope he is all that you promised he would be. For both your sakes."

He chuckled, pulling her swiftly forward, forcing her into a trot to keep up with his pace. After a few minutes, every step caused pain to shoot from her toes to her calf. As they approached the end of the corridor, she saw the steps, her feet screaming in agony. They marched up one enormous flight of stairs, bringing them to their own private viewing area where she immediately removed the shoes for a short reprieve.

"This is a suite or box seats, I think they called them," he motioned to her as if the grandness of the area would make her swoon. "It is private on this side of the glass. They cannot see us, but we can still view all the action." He pointed to two large monitor walls where a two-dimensional or three-dimensional image could be projected. "Or you can view it live from the seats out here." He walked to the glass and slid it open with a wave to reveal a set of dining tables with two chairs situated at each of them. "All we have to do is call for what we want, and we can make an entire evening out of it." He waved his hand again and the door to the balcony closed. "I thought we might be able to take advantage of some privacy this evening." He gave her a sly grin. "I don't know about you, but the arena makes me feel virile and strong. The action makes it very seductive, especially the love stories." He winked at her. "I hear arena boy is very handsome. I imagine he will be set into the romance track. I hope you prepared him for that."

Quinn stared down at her shoes, trying to hide any reactions by slipping them back onto her feet, "Yes, I prepared him for that. He should look weak but end up winning by chance, partial strength, partial smarts and partial luck. At least, that's what it should look like if he does what I told him." Quinn reassured him.

"And will he be able to play the romantic lead? That will be crucial unless he wants them to find a way to eliminate him." Pyrious grabbed her arm, wrenching it so much she almost winced. "This boy better deliver or I may have to find another way to get you to sign that contract."

"You know I need to focus to keep him in line and make you the most money possible. I thought you agreed to wait until he was at the nation invites." Quinn said.

"He seems to take a lot of your focus. I don't like it. I should be your focus." Pyrious spat. "There better not be anything going on between you two. You may know the consequences but sometimes, you think you're smarter than you actually are." He threw her arm back at her. "Let that be your only warning." Stepping back, he looked at her and changed his tactic. "It would go a long way, especially with me agreeing to wait, if you would give me that taste I asked you for. I mean, what can it hurt? We don't have to do everything, but we can still do some things." He moved in closer, running his finger down her arm.

She repressed her shiver of disgust as she didn't want him to think she trembled for him, "What would a taste include?" she asked coyly.

"Oh, well. I suppose we could just start something and then see when we hit a line where you are uncomfortable."

"Not a good enough answer. I want exact limitations, so I can hold you to them or you may just take liberties I wouldn't want you to take before the new agreement goes into effect." Quinn shook her head.

"Wait! Did you sign the contract?" Pyrious asked.

She sighed, trying not to groan in disgust. "After I met with the notary and lawyer and the lawyer made the changes I asked for." She pulled the document out of her bag and plopped it onto the coffee table as Pyrious slid onto the couch, motioning for her to join him.

"Changes. I didn't authorize any changes." He eyed her up and down.

"I know. I did. I signed this copy of the contract. I have mine somewhere safe where you can't mess with it. So, if you choose to sign this version, then we have a deal."

"What changes did you make?" he scowled at the idea.

"Just the roll out date and that you can't be with anyone between now and then." She smiled slyly. "Oh, and you can't make any overt moves or ask for any more tastings until the future roll out date or I am free and clear of all debts I owe to you and free to leave your employ."

"Those are not fair to me." Pyrious was unable to control his tone as his anger rose.

"Before you think you can punish me for that, the changes also include a clause for me to protect myself from you should I decide you are too violent. And there may be something in there claiming this doesn't transfer to any of your sons upon your untimely death, should it occur before the contract is at full maturation."

Pyrious stood straight up, raising his fist, "I cannot believe your gall. You really do think you're smarter than you actually are. You are insane if you think I am signing that."

She waved a finger at his fist and shook her head, stepping toward him gracefully, she pushed him back on the couch. Straddling him, she put her hands on his shoulders and leaned into his ear, "I imagine you've been waiting for a reason. You want me as more than just your toy answering to your every whim. I know you think I am special and I have to wonder," she ran her finger down his chest, tracing the line of his buttons, "Am I really that different from all the rest if you just can't seem to give me the time I need to make us all an enormous fortune."

He groped her ass, grabbing it tightly and pushed it forward gently hoping she would grind against him, but she broke out of his grasp and stood up instead.

"Now, let's see if your actions match your words. You say I'm special. Prove it."

She strode out onto the balcony, leaving him seething on the couch. The intro music started. Placing her bag on the table, she called for a glass of red wine, feeling it was appropriate as eventually, many of these contestants would be fed to the machine for entertainment.

The beginning ceremonies were no different here as the other arenas she visited. The same marching and biographies displayed. Then the contestants went to their separate camps, waiting for their partner name to be pulled, which decided the order of who came out when. How could people not see this couldn't be random to pull off the last- minute staging?

Luca's name was drawn last and it wasn't like the only girl in the field didn't know this was going to happen. There were no other choices, but she acted as if it was a surprise despite production filling her in on what they wanted. It was a classic move for the people the producers thought would lose first to be the last ones to parade during the opening. But this position would only help her plan. Last meant longer odds and better payouts when Luca outperformed expectations.

Pyrious refused to join her as he read over the new contract. Luca's partner ran across the field to meet him. He embraced her tightly then gave her a kiss on the forehead. Their eyes met for a moment and then, he kissed her on the lips. Quinn wanted to stand straight up and shout at him. How could he act this way in front of her? Anger seeped into her every thought.

The arena's speakers blasted the words from the field throughout the space. "My name is Sasha. I know we just met but you're so sexy, I can't wait to get into your pants," she murmured as the crowd cooed at the sight of them and the announcer made comments about how they had become close during training.

"Training." Quinn threw up her hands. "They're not even in the same building for training. Are they bunking in the same room? I doubt it. They're in two different establishments at night and during the day. And really, you can't get that involved with someone after maybe two days of grueling challenges. Ugh!" She slammed back into the chair, folding her arms defiantly.

The exhibition round was getting ready to start.

Quinn sighed, her boredom catching up to her. Knowing Luca would be near the end of the line-up, so they could catch some 'behind the scenes' romance footage of Luca and his new girlfriend Sasha, even in her head the name came out nasally and obnoxious. How was she going to get through the next four rounds of arena with this relationship constantly flaunted in her face?

She really didn't want to watch him paw all over some other woman while she did all she could to stave off Pyrious until finals in the Dome.

Suddenly, Quinn finally realized what had upset Luca so much that day. This was exactly how he felt when he read her contract. Now she understood what he meant about not wanting to share her and at the same time, it made her want him more than she ever wanted anything. She had to claim him as her own, so she would not react this way...or would the reaction be worse? Somehow it didn't matter to her. She *was* ready to be with him. After a week apart, it was time, especially if he was going to have to parade around with that Sasha woman on his arm throughout the competition.

Seventeen

Luca walked into the arena, arm in arm with Sasha. They wore coordinating bands on their wrists, ankles and foreheads that made them look a little geeky but didn't take away from Luca's charm. His smile could melt the nation and it melted Quinn. She gasped when she realized he had no idea what was about to happen. This wasn't normal.

While the cuffs made it easier to control their holographic avatar, it relayed the pain of every hit directly to the contestant. These specific cuffs were usually put into play in later regional rounds, never in exhibition. Quinn thought she would have more time to prepare Luca for this obstacle. What a dreadful change.

Hopefully, he had learned some things during their training sessions because enough electric shock could make a person pass out and give them brain damage. She'd seen it many times before. Hopefully Luca would be able to execute the plan. Quinn grimaced at the thoughts.

After the cheers from the crowd died down, he pushed the button on his wrist, and his avatar was projected in the middle of the arena. A hush fell over the crowd. His avatar was different from anything even Quinn had seen before. Why had she trusted him to create his own? He apparently needed a lot of guidance, and she never gave it to him. She was too busy reveling in his abs and his lips. She breathed a sigh of relief as she realized Pyrious was still pouting inside, not paying attention to the screens. If he saw Luca's crazy avatar, he may just throw her off this balcony for not keeping a closer eye on arena boy.

The avatar was strange and looked pathetic, as if Luca had no idea what he was doing, which was part of the plan, but she wasn't sure if this made it too obvious.

A competitor could pick any attributes in the data base; Luca picked some interesting ones. His appeared with the torso of a gorilla complete with armor chest plate, the head of a wolf with the eyes of a hawk, snout of a hyena and teeth of a tiger, most of it covered except the ears in a battle helmet. The bottom half of the body was from some sort of bear. The claws looked ominous and the legs were wrapped in silver leg armor. The wings of an albatross flanked the gorilla torso's back. A sword in one hand and a shield in the other finished off the look. It was not only original but weirdly interesting and grotesque.

Quinn knew each attribute Luca chose would respond the way it would if it were the animal in question. With that thought, she took a closer look at each of his choices. The ears of a wolf would give him a hearing advantage while the legs of the bear would be able to carry the weight and be faster than expected, maybe even fast enough to take off with those wings, giving him hidden advantages no one would have considered. Hawk eyes were sharp and had more peripheral vision than a man.

Gorilla arms were longer than a man's but worked about the same, giving him the opportunity for greater reach and strength with each blow without a learning curve. The closer she looked, the more she realized he had given this more thought than even she had or any other contestant she'd ever seen. However, the crowd seemed to align with her initial reaction. After a full minute of stunned silence, the arena filled with laughter, jeers and pointing fingers.

The visuals zoomed in on Sasha as she blushed and hung her head. The crowd cackled and heckled Luca's avatar for much longer than they should, but the stream producers probably loved the controversy. Pyrious came out onto the balcony and looked at the arena.

"That's a lot of laughter," he raised an eyebrow at Quinn. "If you wanted people to underestimate him, that avatar seems to have done the trick." He slammed the contract down on the table. "I just hope they don't see him as too much of a fool and refuse to bet on him."

"You set the right odds after this exhibition and they'll bet. They'll think he's the luckiest son of a bitch on the planet," Quinn grinned. "Especially with that choice in avatar."

"Seriously. What was your point to this, Frankenstein's monster,he put together?" Pyrious leaned in, putting a hand on the table but staring at her chest.

"You'll see," she leaned away from him. "Just watch."

As Sasha's avatar appeared in the arena, the laughter changed to tears. She had chosen a female Samurai warrior with full, authentic armor. The other two contestants regained their composure having been overtaken by laughter as well. When all the noise had died down, the pair of opponents turned on their avatars. One was a centaur with a sword, shield, a whip tied to his side and a minimal amount of body armor. The other was a ninja with sharp weapons of various types tucked away in any place available. The ninja flipped and dove and kicked to warm-up while the centaur trotted, no doubt reacting as its controller attempted to understand how to control it. Luca visibly chuckled when he saw the centaur owner on all fours practicing.

Sasha's Samurai did not do flips, as she was not a skilled gymnast, but she was very good at sword play, slashing it around and moving about with precision and grace. All Luca did was beat on his chest and open his mouth to yell, in response the avatar beat on its gorilla chest and released some cat-like sound from its mouth, forcing another eruption of laughter from the audience as he looked just as ridiculous as the cat call from the sidelines.

Every avatar but Luca's shook their head and looked down at their feet, shoulders bouncing a little as they laughed quietly but Luca appeared unphased by the response.

Luca walked around and his avatar followed clumsily. He practiced jumping and running, trying to use his claws to stop and plant his feet. The harder he tried, the clumsier he became, the avatar falling forward and backward often, causing another eruption of laughter and chatter from the seats. Quinn could see this display left Pyrious unimpressed, and his annoyance was beginning to show.

"Are you trying to make a fool out of me? Get the best of me? Assert your own power and independence?" he growled at her.

"I did that with the contract. You just need to wait and watch. We've trained for all this," she lied, praying Pyrious couldn't tell.

Quinn worried. Could Luca, despite the thought behind his avatar, be able to master moving it around the arena enough to win? If he did, would the victory look like a dash of luck as opposed to actual skill? While she appreciated his efforts, she knew the outcome would have to be positive for him to stay in the competition and for her to keep her body to herself.

A loud buzz sounded around the arena. The match had begun. Sasha battled the ninja avatar with her Samurai as they were more closely matched. While she was agile and combat ready, the ninja's controller seemed to have some extra acrobatic skills, making it more difficult for Sasha to land any blows. She spent most of the time chasing and ducking things being thrown at her until finally, a throwing star lodged into her avatar's forehead. The Samurai flickered, disappearing a moment later, leaving Luca to contend with the ninja if he managed to dispatch the Centaur creature first.

As Sasha fell to the ground, twitching as the crowd roared in approval, Luca lumbered toward the Centaur, who removed his whip from his side after sheathing the sword. With the flick of the wrist, the whip hit the torso and Luca's monster stumbled back a few steps. Lowering his shield, Luca left only enough of a view to see the Centaur, who slashed the whip at him again, making the shield vibrate. Luca's sheath was inside the shield, and the Centaur didn't notice him put it away. Then Luca charged the Centaur who managed to whip the shield again before the full force of the shield hit the Centaur square across his front, barreling it backward into the wall.

Unfortunately, the force sent Luca's combo creature flying backward, landing square on his wings. One looked broken while the avatar let out a grunt, like the wind was knocked out of it. The ninja came at Luca with a flying leap. All Luca could do to avoid the blow as roll, forcing him to temporarily release the shield. Recovering as quickly as he could, his ears and eyes helped him see the flying daggers headed in his direction. Luca rolled away again, stopping on his belly and pushing himself up to his knees to get back on his feet.

He heard the Centaur recover and speed in his direction. Luca crawled to his shield, skidding across the ground as he couldn't stop the forward momentum. The body he'd created was too heavy to stop that quickly. Quinn covered her eyes as she watched the Centaur bear down on Luca's backside. Suddenly, Luca rolled over and fiddled with the sheathed sword, pulling it out just as the Centaur reached him and slit the Centaur across the entire bottom of the body.

The surprise on Luca's face showed on the screens as the Centaur flickered and disappeared, symbolizing the blow would have killed the creature. Quinn doubted Luca had acted completely by chance, but she wasn't sure. As he recovered, the ninja managed go throw a dart at him. The needle buried itself into the back of Luca's hand forcing the sword to clatter on the ground as it moved straight through his palm.

Luca scowled. Now the hand didn't respond. In no time, the ninja punctured a calf and his arm. Then, the ninja avatar pulled out two swords from its back and ran toward Luca's creature. Luca struggled but couldn't get up. He heard and saw the ninja adjust and fly toward the gorilla chest. Reflexively, Luca rolled onto his back and put his legs up in the air. The ninja landed on the enormous bear paws, complete with massive claws. Luca kicked and kicked, bouncing the ninja up and rolling it over and over as the claws cut the protective gear to shreds and started digging into skin and flesh.

The ninja's controller tried desperately to regain control of their avatar but to no avail. Luca batted it around like a beach ball until it started to flicker. The audience gasped as the ninja bounced up in the air one last time and disappeared. Luca's humorous monstrosity turned out to be more formidable than anyone realized.

Pyrious' grin spread from ear to ear, "He is one lucky son of a bitch. That kid lucked out in this match, but I don't know if his luck will last."

"I told you. I trained him to make it look like he had little skill and most of his good fortune was strictly by chance," she stood and tilted her head with a smile. "You set the odds accordingly." She strode toward the main room. "Let the guard know I'm headed down as your emissary. That is, unless you don't want to sponsor him?"

"Go. I must go back and immediately set the odds. People will want them out tonight after this showing. Besides, he needs some more coaching. I have no interest in the opening banquet either. Everyone from this district looks at me like some sort of criminal. Just be home by dawn." Pyrious sneered. He seemed a bit off his game. Quinn hoped he was still reeling from the new contract.

Eighteen

Quinn entered the training grounds, instructing the guard to escort her to Luca's assigned quarters. The security guard rolled his eyes. This was too common place of a request for him to refuse but Quinn knew he never thought she would ever be the one asking in Pyrious's place. They knew each other well and when she noticed the look on his face, she rolled her eyes and smiled.

"I'm scouting and recruiting." The comment forced a snort and a chuckle from the guard. "In the non-naughty way, you pervert." She shoved into his shoulder.

"Good. For a minute, I thought we'd lost you to the dark side," the guard smiled and pushed her back a little. "I was lost to the darkness long before you ever got this job," she lamented, not meaning to be so honest. "Clearly, I can see that," he motioned toward her body. "You've had some work done."

"Not my choice," she grumbled. The guard stopped walking, putting his hand out to stop her, concern written all over his face. She put him off. "Really, I don't want to talk about it."

"Well, no offense, but I imagine the work you've had done will make it easier to recruit. I mean, I remember you when you came through before but somehow, with the imperfections, you're even better looking."

She punched the guard in the shoulder, forcing a wince as she shook her head. The guard started moving again, motioning to the door she needed to knock on.

Raising her fist, she knocked three times and waited. As the door swung open, her eyes widened. Sasha stood on the other side, clearly tipsy, with a glass of wine in her hand.

Quinn gaped before she heard Luca coming to the door, "I told you not to answer." He was behind Sasha now, a little tipsy himself. "I wasn't expecting..." His voice trailed off and his eyes grew as wide as Quinn's when he saw her at the door. "Quinn!" He grabbed the wine from Sasha and ran to set it down on the table. "I...uh...wasn't really. This isn't what you think." He looked over his shoulder at the ladies in the doorway. As he turned back and saw them both looking at him expectantly, his eyes fell to the floor. "We were just..."

Sasha turned to her, "We were just getting to know one another a little better for the show. You know, the love thing. It helps if we know a bit about one another." Sasha added, "It's all part of the game. We wouldn't want to upset the producers." Sasha grinned at Quinn before turning and kissing Luca on the cheek. "And I can say that I am pleased with their choice. At least he's cute."

Quinn felt her temperature rise and was almost certain her face went livid. Luca, eyes wide in the shock, watched as Quinn gripped the door frame and her knuckles went white.

"Sasha, this is Quinn. We met..." he stumbled as Quinn and Sasha glared at him. "Before the exhibition. She's here to talk to me about a sponsorship." Quinn raised an eyebrow at him, "And I don't think we should ever do that again. We need to stay focused and objective," Luca danced a little as he cleared his throat. "You know, for the story line we've been assigned, Sasha." He dipped his head at Sasha giving him a stern look.

Quinn took this opportunity to move into the room, and she put a hand on Sasha's shoulder, "So, dearie, what he's saying here is it's time for you to go. We have business to conduct and frankly, you're not a part of it."

Sasha turned on her heel and suddenly stood nose to nose with Quinn, "Maybe I should be, sweetie. As you can clearly see, we make quite team." Sasha sneered at Quinn.

Luca looked from one woman to the other, hand over his mouth, eyes bulging.

"Actually, sweetie," Quinn seethed through her teeth. "From what I saw in the match today, Luca managed winning all by himself." She smiled at Luca as he slowly backed up to the chair to sit and watch. "And I'm certain Luca would like to talk business with me this evening."

Luca shifted his gaze off them and shook his head. Quinn hoped he knew this issue with Sasha would end with one of them dead. He'd better be sure which one would win.

"I hate to be the bearer of bad news, honey, but that was mostly planned. He wanted to look stronger than he thought he did after the laughter. And obviously it worked, because you're here to offer him a sponsorship, something we both desperately need," Sasha smirked. "So, since we're a team, he won't accept a sponsorship if you don't offer me one too."

Quinn's knuckles went white again as she formed fists. Luca stood immediately, rushing to put himself between them. Shouldering in, he faced Sasha.

"Sasha, I never said anything like that, and you can't speak for me. This is just a story line from the producing council. You know this," Luca gave her a stern look, gripping her by the shoulders.

"Luca. Luca. Luca." Sasha ran her fingers up his chest and smiled at his reaction. "Baby, there is no reason we can't be together, for real, not just in a story. I know we'd at least have a little fun."

"Sasha, I think you're really nice," Luca started. Quinn stared at him, but he refused to look back at her, "But I'm not sure this was a good idea. I don't want to do something we both may regret later."

"Why would I regret getting a catch like you?" Sasha pushed him back into Quinn, forcing Quinn to fall onto the floor.

Luca turned to Quinn who scowled at Sasha. He knelt to help her up. "Sasha, you need to go! You are ruining my chance at a legitimate sponsorship. I don't care if you need one too. This is my shot and I won't let you ruin it." After helping Quinn to a seat, he turned back to Sasha, "You need to go," he led Sasha by the arm to the door. "Now!" He pushed her out into the hall and slammed the door in her face.

Quinn figured Sasha pouted on the other side of the door for a moment. Because soon enough Sasha pounded on it until it opened again. This time, Quinn answered the door. Sasha's anger met her on sight.

Quinn smiled. "Sweetie, now you just look desperate. Don't make me call the guard," Quinn stood casually in the doorway. She and Luca stared at Sasha for a long while. Sasha grunted, stomping her feet and throwing her hands in the air, like a two-year-old tantrum before turning and walking down the hall.

Nineteen

"Really? Seven days? We're apart for seven days and you're ready to crawl down her pants? I can't believe I fell for your bull shit!" As Quinn began to pace, Luca fell into a chair, resting his forehead on his hands.

"I knew I should've kept this professional." Quinn ranted. "I can't believe I trusted you. Dropped my guard. I don't trust anyone. What was I thinking?" She dropped onto the couch. "Of course, you were just appeasing me to get you where you wanted to go. How could I be so blind? How could you do this to me?!" The last sentence screamed through her lips although she had not intended it to ever exit her lips or be that loud.

"I'm not sure what just happened. She showed up here with wine and wanted to talk." Luca groaned, knowing Quinn wouldn't believe his side of the story. "I've never had wine before. I thought it was grape juice. I didn't know it could make me feel...like this." Luca shook his head and looked at Quinn, who remained sitting on the couch, turned away from him, mumbling to herself. "I didn't know anything would happen or what she wanted." He looked at her desperately. "My head is so fuzzy. If I had known, I never would have let her in." Quinn harrumphed and still refused to look at him. "Seriously Quinn, I had no idea any of that would happen and if I had known it would break you..."

"Break me!" She stood up, turning, standing so close she towered over him. "What the hell does that mean? You can't break me."

Locking eyes, Luca grimaced, "You're right," he smirked a little. "Because you're already broken."

Quinn swung the back of her hand at him. With skill, he blocked her blow by grabbing her wrist but there was enough power on it to push him sideways in his seat.

"You're an asshole!" She shouted.

"And you're a pretentious snob who thinks she's better than me because she managed to get herself inside the Dome walls." Luca spouted. "And this is the only way to get you to listen or notice me!"

Quinn looked at him hard. Luca could imagine her thoughts. Did he use Sasha to set her up? Was anything he just said true?

"I'm leaving!" she wrenched free of his grip and took a step toward the door.

He stood up, moving in close behind her, whispering tersely in her ear, "No you're not. You have to settle this, or I'll bomb out of the next fight and Pyrious will be so angry with you."

"The only man who has a tiny ability to control me is Pyrious. You can't be him or do what he does. You don't have it in you." Quinn barked back.

"What makes you think so?" he replied coyly, pulling her back by her hips.

"Because if you could, I wouldn't have caught you out here with Sasha. I would have caught you naked and you would have let it happen."

"Is that what you think? This was all a ploy to get you angry or hot and bothered?" He loved the smell of her hair, filling his nose with it as he inhaled, "You're right. I am not that crafty. Letting her in here was a mistake, one I will not repeat, but at least you get it now. Why I can't handle sharing you."

"I got it when you were all over her in the arena," Quinn barked, pulling away from him and turning around.

"I honestly didn't mean for any of this to happen, Quinn. The wine...it made my head fuzzy." His look pleaded with her to believe him. "It makes it hard to think."

"You expect me to believe you have never had an alcoholic drink before?" Quinn folded her arms. "Really?"

Shaking his head at her, "Aren't I the guy who came to you to get more Digicreds? You think someone who can't scrape by on Govcreds can afford a drop of alcohol?" He finished by raising an eyebrow at her. He knew she hated that, but he did it anyway. To her, it meant he'd managed to one up her or she wasn't right but this time Quinn chose to be the embodiment of stubborn, and would not give him the satisfaction of being right this time, even if he made sense.

Sure enough, Quinn snarled, "I know there's more going on with the two of you than you want me to know. I watched you in the arena. You like her more than you should."

He moved in close again, wrapping his arm around her waist as she struggled against him, "I pretended she was you." The comment made her freeze. She looked stunned. Clearly she hadn't thought of that.

"But she was here, and you kissed her," Quinn's voice sounded weak.

"Correction. She kissed me." He wrapped her up with both arms now. "Did I smile or close my eyes? Did I do anything to indicate I wanted or even attempted to kiss her back?"

Quinn looked at Luca through the corners of her eyes and pursed her lips as she pushed him away. "I can't know what was happening in your head as I watched, but you did look really funny when she kissed you. Your arms were flailing and the look on your face..." Unable to contain herself, she burst into a hysterical fit of laughter like Luca had never seen.

"What's so funny?"Luca was confused.

"If only there was a mirror in front of you when it happened. Then you could under..." she started to laugh harder. "Then you could..." Tears flowed from her eyes. She waved her hands, trying to recover. "It's like you'd never kissed anyone before. You looked so..." the laughter returned as she dropped to her knees, grabbing her stomach. "awkward. You...so...awkward!" She could barely breath as she laughed even harder than before while Luca watched.

A yawn overtook Luca and he decided he'd been made fun of for long enough. "I'm heading to bed. When you're done amusing yourself, you can have the couch. I'll get up early and we can talk strategy and other things."

"Luca. Wait." Quinn reached out to him with one hand, but the laughter and tears still flowed. "I'm sorry. I think."

Frowning, he shook his head. "I'll see you in the morning."

"No really, wait, Luca," the laughter died down as she managed to get to her feet. "Really, I'm done now, and we need to talk."

"My performance today was fine. I did what you said and made most of it look lucky." Luca spat at her.

"I didn't mean to hurt your feelings. Really. But I know today was mostly luck. I trained you, remember." Quinn said.

"As much as it's been fun to have you laugh at me incessantly and now criticize my performance, it's more than I can take this evening. Maybe it's the wine talking but perhaps we really do need to keep this professional. I can't handle anything beyond that right now."

"Luca, now you're just being a wet rag, all drippy and droopy and sad. If you can't handle a little teasing," she grinned from ear to ear.

"I don't know about you but tonight has not been a barrel full of laughs and fun. Wine is the worst. I am never drinking again." Luca whined, waving her off as he headed to his bed chamber.

She followed him to his room and stood in the doorway. He didn't bother to shoo her away as he pulled off his clothes.

Smiling, she moved to the end of his bed. "Luca, I'm sorry for hurting your feelings. I wish there was something I could do to make you feel better."

He glared at her before pulling down the covers and climbing into bed. "There is no need. I understand how things have to be now for us to work together. If you've got an itch, have Pyrious scratch it."

Quinn sucked in a breath. He knew those words had stung her, deep.

She scowled at him. "I managed to stall him until the end of the national arena for your group." She looked sickened at the thought. "Besides, he isn't what I think about when I think about my future or, well, other things."

"Strictly professional. That's what you said before, right? Now I agree with you." Luca stretched and buried himself into the soft bed.

"Hey, I don't like you when you've been drinking. You turn into a jerk. Seriously, all the stuff you said out there to me and you're mad at me for laughing at you?" Quinn slammed a fist into the bed. "We weren't very nice to each other. How about we just agree not to pick on one another, no matter the circumstance. Okay?"

"Whatever you say, Quinn." he mumbled.

She ripped the blanket off of him, tossing it behind her. "You are so frustrating! Can't we have a simple communication without you acting like a complete child?"

Luca shot up, sitting on the bed looking at her, reading the distress shown on her face. He couldn't help but smile at making her feel the same way he just did, causing a chuckle.

"Now what is so funny?" She hissed at him.

"You," he smiled. "You're so determined to get your way, you don't even realize you haven't listened to anything I've said. Talk about a one-track mind."

"What do you mean? I heard you and I acknowledged you. You're the one acting all stuck up!" Quinn folded her arms defiantly.

"Let's just agree to forget everything that happened earlier and start over. Okay?" Luca put his hands up defensively. He knew when Quinn had her mind set on something, she could kill to get it.

"That sounds fair." She walked around the bed, extending her hand for him to shake.

Instead, he grabbed her hand and pulled her to him, launching her onto the bed with her legs sprawled across his lap. She shrieked as she flew.

"It's rare I can take you by surprise," he smiled at her. "Now, what was it you wanted to talk about?" Looking deep into her eyes, he caressed her face.

"Your avatar for starters. Where the hell did you get that bright idea?" She looked at him sternly.

"It worked didn't it? Made me look stupid but proved to be formidable?" Luca replied. "That was what we discussed, right?" He put his hands up to indicate he was innocent. "I'm just following your plan but if you want me to stop..."

She socked him in the arm. He winced and rubbed his new hurt spot. It would bruise. Quinn slid onto the bed to face him.

"You have to be more careful. Those bands will shock you in the future." Quinn pointed as she tried to be serious.

"They shock you?" Luca looked horrified.

"Yes. When you take damage. They shock you. If you're not careful, the shocks can knock you out long before your avatar gets a kill shot."

"Why would they do that?" he looked at her confused.

"The producers way of controlling the outcome. They can decide how powerful the shocks are in the moment. They can punish you that way too. If you kill someone off too quickly or find a way to make them look bad to the board." She explained.

"I will keep that in mind," he replied, looking just as serious as she sounded. "Is that how some of the competitors end up with brain damage?"

"It's one of the reasons why they don't tell anyone. They allow you to find out through experience. It also adds an edge to the game for the watchers in the Dome because they know you're getting shocked." Quinn played with the sheet as she spoke. "But you can't act like you know because, well the guards know I'm here."

"The guards know you're here? Won't we get into trouble? Won't that get me charged with cheating and expelled from competition?" Luca looked at her, knowing she had to see the worry written in his eyes.

"No. This is perfectly normal." She said.

"How is this normal?" Luca asked.

"It's normal for regents and officials or their representatives, like me, to come into the training station and visit competitors. They're assuming we're making a sponsorship deal. Some have more nefarious ideas and act on them. Probably why Sasha wanted out of her room." She frowned at him. "Many of us stay until the next morning to protect our assets and the producers and guards assume what they will."

"What do you mean, something more nefarious," he moved in closer. She had to know the idea would turn him on. "Do you have nefarious motives, Miss Quinn?"

"Perhaps my motives are not purely linked to sponsorship, and you look like you may be amenable to that discussion." She looked him up and down. "Based on your various stages of undress, I would say we are now at an opportune moment."

Leaning in and cradling his face with both hands, she kissed him, forcing her tongue between his lips. Something she hadn't done before. It took Luca aback but intrigued him at the same time. Climbing on top of him, they laid back in the bed, locked together as his hands made their way down her back and to her hips. She broke away, looking at him and smiling.

He needed to be sure. "You have me at a distinct disadvantage. You're mostly clothed and I have nothing to bargain with." Shaking her head, she rolled off him and laid on her back next to him, trying not to chuckle. "Well, Miss Quinn, what is your sponsorship offer?"

"I don't know what will make you choose us over someone else. Others will send women prettier than I am and much more willing to please you in many ways," answered Quinn.

"Really. They do that?" Luca rolled over supporting his head on his hand. "I didn't know..."

"Yes really. They will offer you the world. Maybe not in the first level, but as you move up, you'll be propositioned more and more and some aren't as discreet as I am." She grabbed his free hand, "But you have to be careful. Making enemies with someone outside the arena can cost you. Many of them have producers on their payroll and one word from them and they will do everything they can to remove you."

Twenty

The sun broke through the curtains as the air from the cooler glided across the room from underneath the window. Stretching as she sat up, Quinn looked at Luca longingly. He sprawled out across the bed. She knew it was three times the size of any bed he'd ever seen before. Part of her regretted more didn't happen last night but another part of her was happy they hadn't done anything yet. She knew she wasn't truly ready for sex with anyone but if Luca had managed to upset her any more than he had the night before, she would have done almost anything to shut him up. To teach him a lesson. Taking in a deep breath, she dialed the phone for breakfast. Today would start another week of training for Luca and Sasha while the other round of competitors had their exhibition matches in the local arena.

Luca would be available all week to do whatever he pleased but it was suggested they train as much as possible. Quinn would only help him at night. During the day, he would range free and as it was obvious from the previous night's activities, Sasha had her eye on him, possibly wanting to make their story line as true to life as possible.

Sasha must not be very skilled because she was pinning her hopes on the story line and the producers intervening on her behalf if she couldn't get a good enough sponsorship. Quinn knew as well as anyone how hard it could be to balance life outside the arena with life inside the arena. Sasha was in a fight for her very survival and couldn't be faulted for taking advantage of every avenue available to her.

"What are you doing?" Luca groaned, reaching across the bed trying to coerce her back under the covers, hoping she would be more amenable to taking things a little further.

"Ordering breakfast," said Quinn.

Luca sat up like a shot, "Then people will know you're here. Pyrious will know you're here."

"I told you, this is normal. You'll get to check your acting chops because you'll have to pretend like we did more than talk last night and I have to give you liberty to treat me as you please." She put her hand over the receiver just in case someone on the other side picked up. "And I have made it abundantly clear to Pyrious that I don't do those things. He usually uses escorts for intimate acts with his contestants but there will be a buzz that he's serious about picking you up and Pyrious rarely bets on a loser. So, using me will ensure the betting on you will go through the roof." She kept eyes on him as she ordered. He wasn't paying attention. She must have made his head spin at all the possibilities. She was back beside him on the bed again before he noticed. She touched his forehead. "It's the wine. It's called a hangover. I've ordered you something to help with that. In the meantime, you need to hydrate."

She kissed him on the cheek and turned to crawl out of bed. Despite what disorientation and pain he felt, Luca responded by grabbing her arm and pulling her back into his lap. She smiled and broke his grasp, climbing out of bed again only to have him pull her back in.

"What is it you think you're going to get out of me this morning?" Quinn asked, somehow back in Luca's lap.

"Just another kiss, like last night," Luca grinned from ear to ear.

"I'm surprised you remembered. That was after quite a bit of alcohol," Quinn smirked.

"Please, just one before I have to act like a complete slime ball. I mean, I want to know if I smack you on the rear that you're not going to hate me later." He chuckled.

Her eyes narrowed at him, "Doing any such thing will cause you a great deal of pain later. This I guarantee." Quinn no longer smiled at him. "And you can't think the other patrons won't know how I normally act. I am NOT an escort."

She leaned in and their lips met. Tingles ran down her spine as he pulled her in closer. She drank in his scent and his taste. Luca did too, his tongue longing for more. When she pulled away, he pulled her back in, leaning back down onto the bed. His hands gripping her tightly as she writhed on top of him, he was enjoying himself and focused on taking advantage of every minute of her company. Unzipping her dress, she pulled it over her head without hesitation and leaned back into him.

They heard the knock at the door. It was breakfast. She hopped off him, agilely avoiding his attempts to get her back into bed and on top of him.

"I'm coming," Quinn shouted through the bedroom door as the knocking persisted.

Luca watched her, wanting more but unsure how to ask for it. They had agreed to take it slow, and she had managed to stall Pyrious for over two months. She really was an amazing catch, and he was fairly certain he was falling in love with her. He hoped she felt the same, but they hadn't really discussed their feelings. Neither of them wanted this to be complicated and the discussion about sex would be complicated.

Quinn hung on the door as the man walked in with the tray and unloaded it onto the table. He smiled at her, looking her up and down and then raised his eyebrows.

"Knock it off. You know I don't do that. I just fell asleep," she snarled.

The waiter didn't say a word, only smiled and shook his head. Luca also knew she didn't behave that way. It was easier since she knew most of the people who worked in this arena. She had explained to him that it had been a long time since she had been back.

"I'll just start the coffee and tea in the kitchen, and I'll be out of your way," the server said stepping toward the kitchen as Luca walked out in only his boxers, not bothering to put on a robe himself. It was time to act.

"SHUT THE DOOR," LUCA commanded as he walked toward Quinn. She followed his direction and when she turned around, he wrapped his arm around her waist, pushing her up against the door and kissing her so passionately, even she forgot it was for show, wrapping her arms around his neck and even biting his lip a little.

"Thank you for ordering breakfast." He whispered against her neck. Releasing her, he walked toward the bedroom again as she felt plastered to the door, her entire body singing his praises. "I'm hopping in the shower. You can't eat until I come out and make sure the server finds a way to keep it warm. I hate a cold breakfast." He smiled over his shoulder with a twinkle in his eye as he walked through the bedroom door.

Quinn breathed in deep. His scent still lingered in the air. The server had walked back into the room and now raised an eyebrow at her.

"Oh, shut up! He's cute!" she blushed and watched the floor all the way to the bedroom.

She heard the main door close as she checked the knob for the bathroom. Luca had actually locked the door. Pouting, she stomped to the bed to figure out how she could torture him the way he had just tortured her. She grinned and got to work. Before long, he came out in his towel. "This has always been my favorite view of you," she said. "At least of all the ones I've seen so far."

She sat on the bed without her dress on. He approached her and tried to pull her up, his hair dripping onto her lap. Refusing to stand, she removed his towel and pulled him in her direction instead. They laid side by side, kissing and touching one another until their arousal was at its peak. Quinn lifted herself away and looked him up and down, smiling. When he tried to haul her in for another round, she popped off the bed.

"Well, you know you hate your breakfast to be cold. We best eat now." Smiling with a twinkle in her eye as she walked toward the dining room.

From the corner of her eye she watched him roll onto his back and groan, running his hands through his hair. He muttered, "You will be the death of me, woman."

Quinn grinned. He would enjoy every minute of the ride. She'd guarantee it.

"You better get out here before it gets cold," she teased.

Not bothering to get dressed, Luca walked into the main room and sat next to her at the dining table. A spread of juice on ice, coffee, tea, toast, fruits and yogurt were visible, with a few more plates yet to be revealed. Quinn smiled even wider at him and handed him a plate, taking the cover off a bowl full of eggs, a plate of sausage and bacon and her favorite, pancakes and waffles.

"You're spoiling me," he also smiled at the spread and began to fill his plate.

"No worries. You only have to pay it back if you don't make it to the Dome. Too bad you don't have a sponsor. If you had a sponsor, then they would pay for it whether or not you make it to the Dome. Part of the agreement and the fine print I am sure you didn't read when you signed your competition contract."

"Damn, they always get you with the fine print. Guess I better just win it all then, huh?" he took a swig of juice, wiping his mouth with the back of his hand.

"Oh, we need to work on your manners." She stood up, grabbing a napkin and reached over to him, wiping his mouth with it. "You use these to clean your face at the table."

He grabbed her hips and pulled her over him. Now she straddled him as she cleaned his lips. He slid his chair forward, so he was even closer to her and put his elbows on the table, locking her in place.

"Gah, you're hopeless. Elbows are not allowed on the table. You should never reach for anything. If it isn't close enough, you ask for it to be passed to you. And for heaven's sake, be sure to chew with your mouth closed. The banquet tonight will show how sophisticated you are to the producer panel. Everyone wants to know how well you will fit in with the others in the Dome."

"No reaching," his eyes were twinkling again as he reached around her, pulling her flush against his bare chest. "You mean, like this?" She grinned at him. "Would you please bring yourself closer to me?"

He lifted and shifted their bodies. This put the table top against the back of her thighs, and she leaned back on it, half-sitting on the hard surface in response to his request. Luca stood up, moving in, loving his position between her legs. In response, she wrapped her legs around his waist and her arms around his neck.

"I thought you wanted to eat before it got cold." she smiled.

"You told me to act like an asshole. So, I did." Luca smiled back.

"So, you don't mind a cold breakfast?" she asked.

"I don't get breakfast very often and this is more food than I can hope to buy in a week. It would last me all day if they don't take it away." responded Luca.

"Then maybe we should take this somewhere else?" Quinn said.

"Why? Right here will work fine for me." Luca's smile grew wider. "But I want you to be comfortable. This will hurt you. It would be better with some padding."

"I thought you said you'd not been in a serious relationship for a long time." Quinn's eyebrows raised.

"You don't have to be in a serious relationship to have experience." Luca replied.

"Gees, how many women have you been with?" her eyes narrowed at him.

"A handful. And yes, I have been tested and vaccinated just like anyone else." he said.

"Well, I guess you're in luck. My injuries have left me sterile." Quinn sounded sad. "I guess that makes me a bad mate."

"No Quinn, that makes you special." Luca lifted her chin to face him. "That doesn't matter to me."

"You'd say anything to get what you want." she mumbled.

"Have I ever said whatever it takes to get what I want? Is that the person you have come to know?" He stepped back from her. "The decision is yours. We don't have to do anything you don't want to do." She admired his restraint. His arousal had remained strong despite their conversation.

She grabbed his hands before he could get too far away, he shifted back in, "I want this. I do. So much. But I'm not sure..."

"You're not sure if you're ready? That's okay Quinn. It's okay," he kissed her on the forehead.

Holding his face in his hands, their eyes locked on one another. Quinn knew the hunger she felt showed in her eyes. It probably made him want to take her right now, but he'd left the choice up to her. She wrapped her legs around him, kissing him again. Finally, she'd made it difficult to for him to control himself. He lifted her off the table and carried her back to the bed. The training had improved his upper body strength. He held her flush against him from chest to knees as he walked. In the bedroom, he sat her down on the soft bed and stepped back, away from her, before leaning his face in to capture her lips. Time ceased as he kissed her, paused, and then kissed her again.

"It is up to you, but I can't take much more of this," he panted heavily, each kiss taking more of his breath away.

"Okay." Quinn said, just as breathless as Luca.

"What does that mean?" Luca whispered.

"Yes, Luca. Please. I want you. Right now." Quinn said.

"Are you sure?" Luca asked. "You don't have to."

"I want to." Quinn said.

He reached for her scant clothing. Eventually he got the robe off her shoulders. She pushed him away as he struggled to remove her panties, his fingers shaking.

"I'm nervous." He blushed.

"Me too," she said kissing him again.

Twenty-One

It was early evening when Luca finally rolled over and realized Quinn was missing from the bed. Looking around, she was not in the room either.Leaping out of bed, Luca found the robe she had worn earlier on the floor.

Putting it on, he raced around his quarters to find her. The bathroom floor was wet from a shower, and half the breakfast was gone. So was Quinn. Long gone. No note. No notice. No message.

He slumped into a dining room chair, holding his forehead in his hands. She'd abandoned him. The moment of panic opened to sorrow. How had he misread the situation? She was just using him, but he felt something. All this had meant something to him. The more he thought about it, the angrier he became. How could she do this to him?

Before he was thinking straight, he found himself in the training room for this building, beating one of the punching bags until his hands were bruised and almost bloody. Sweat dripped down his face as he worked through his anger and into his frustration. When he reached sadness, he stopped fighting and headed back to his room to shower and forget the day's events.

Still kicking himself for being stupid and expressing everything he had that morning, he ran across Sasha in the hallway. She gave him a hug and a kiss on the cheek. None of it registered. She pulled him further down the hall and into the public room, where they worked on interviews and their story line with the producers until he realized Sasha was telling everyone they had grown so close in such a short amount of time, they were planning on moving into his quarters for the rest of the competition. This forced him into the head producer's office, where the producer explained the rules of shared spaces and arranged for them to move into new quarters with two bedrooms over the next few days.

"Thanks for being so accommodating. It doesn't mean we have to be together but just so you know, I wouldn't mind if we were," gripping him by the arm as they walked, Sasha gushed about how successful they were going to be.

Luca looked at her hand on his arm. He saw bruises on her wrists and when he turned to look at her, there was a bruise on her hairline. Maybe it happened during training, but he doubted it. They looked suspicious and he knew deep down, she'd been attacked in her room last night. The night he sent her away. A plummeting feeling in his stomach forced him to cough to keep him from retching.

"What happened last night? I mean, after you left my room?" Luca asked, his voice laced with concern.

She froze, turning toward him, "Nothing that hasn't happened before. Nothing I shouldn't have expected."

He really should shut down her plans to cohabitate. But she needed protection from whoever was waiting in her room. Damn. Sasha knew him well enough now to know he would protect her even if they weren't together even if he'd let Quinn send her away. That decided things for him. Quinn had sent Sasha away then used him and now Sasha had been attacked. Sasha's wounds were partially his fault. He couldn't have felt worse than he did at this very moment.

"I just want you to know. I'm not looking to be with anyone, but I'll pretend with you as long as we follow the rules," Luca gave her a weak grin. "I'll keep you safe as long as you leave me alone. Don't try to give me anymore wine or anything else."

"Things didn't go so well with your mystery woman last night then?" Sasha suddenly seemed really aggressive. "I would have thought you'd get exactly what you wanted." She gave him a half-smile. "Unless you were expecting something different."

"I really don't want to talk about it. Let's just get our stuff and move into the new quarters. To get it over with. I just want to get out of those quarters all together." Luca rambled even as he wished he could focus. They turned down the corridor toward her room.

He said, "I'll help you if you help me."

Before long, their bags were in much bigger quarters. Two and a half baths with two bedrooms and a full kitchen which meant they could get shopping privileges. Luca checked his feed. His avatar was trending but not all of it was in a positive way. Many people were making fun of the enormous, strange creature but those who had watched the match warned it was more formidable than anyone thought it would be, as he did win the match.

The Theorists and Odds Makers were all talking about him and his avatar as if they were unsure if he was the stupidest man they'd ever seen or the smartest man to ever enter the arena. They were torn because he was older, but they wondered whether he was a deep thinker. Some theorized he was making fun of the entire arena stream with his avatar and that accounted for his age. He'd never felt older than when he checked his feed because everyone was talking about how much older he was than everyone else, even though he was barely in his early twenties.

Before turning in his key to his old quarters to the production office, he stopped in to see if there was anything he may have forgotten. As he walked into the bedroom, he jumped at the sight of Quinn sitting on the bed, waiting for him. He stood, paralyzed by her presence, unsure how to react.

Finally, Quinn broke the silence. "So, you're moving in with Sasha?" she asked. The shocked look on his face was apparently enough to answer her question. She continued, "It's all over the feeds. I'm sure it's part of the story line strategy but since you really didn't say much..."

She stared at the floor, like she was waiting for him to say something...anything.

Suddenly Luca understood. All these weeks with Quinn had taught him more about her than he'd known. In her heart, Quinn hoped to hear it was all for the show, but worried that he did have something with Sasha. He knew what he needed to say. Could he say it the right way? Could he make her understand? The complications of taking things beyond business were here and now.

"She was attacked last night, Quinn. We sent her away and some sponsor or their agent attacked her." Luca blurted out.

Quinn scoffed. "You sent her away and this happened to her?"

"I didn't know that would happen. I know it does happen, but I had no idea she was running from something like that."

Quinn mumbled. "I'm sorry she was attacked." She fidgeted and looked everywhere but at him.

The conversation stagnated awkwardly. Finally Luca cried out, "Where the hell did you go, Quinn? No note. No indication of why you left. I gave you all of me and you left me."

"I didn't leave you," she said defensively. "I have responsibilities other places and I have to keep up the appearance this is a business arrangement. If Pyrious found out..." Quinn shook her head.

"We'd both be dead, I know. But you didn't have to leave like that. I mean, I dozed off for an hour or so. Why couldn't you wait or leave a note or something? Anything was preferable to the feeling of being used and abandoned."

She snapped, "How about coming back as soon as I could only to hear you are moving in with Sasha!" She rose and moved in close, hands on his chest, "I didn't use you. I would never use you. Not like that. I mean, I know I'm using you in other ways." Sighing heavily, "This may be too complicated."

"Maybe we should have just kept it professional." Luca lamented. "Then it would be easier for you."

Quinn wasn't going for it. She countered, "Take me to your new quarters and I'll apologize to Sasha. Then we can train and discuss the strategy with that crazy avatar of yours. I promise I won't do anything remotely cute or..." she backed away from him, looking him up and down, "And you need to be on your best behavior too. Keep it professional."

"Agreed." Even as he said it, Luca wondered how he could make that happen.

Twenty-Two

Luca sat in the waiting area. As he strapped on his gear butterflies sparred and fought like avatars in his stomach. Placing the competition glasses over his eyes, he would wait to switch them on after he launched his avatar. This match meant something, his second chance to prove his avatar's effectiveness. Plus the Centaur would be looking for redemption, and possibly blood, after their first match. No matter what strings Quinn and Pyrious might pull with the producers, there was still no stopping his opponent from causing him pain in the worst ways. That gave Luca courage. Arena fighters were still human and reacted as all people did no matter what forces or problems surrounded them.

He heard his name over the loudspeaker, and he walked toward the end of the tunnel. As he watched his highlight reel from the exhibition match, he realized how lucky he actually had been when he fought the Centaur a week ago. Knowing they had both seen the reels ensured it would be even harder this time around.

"Luca the Lucky!"the voice echoed the name around the arena.

Grimacing at the voice, he raised a hand. He hated the moniker, but he didn't get to choose it. Before he walked on to the arena floor, Sasha met him, giving him a long kiss on camera.

"For luck," she said into the mic, winking at the camera more than him.

The crowd went wild. Their story line had trended so much in the last week, Luca was almost certain he would win this match by sheer force of will from the crowd alone. Across from his tunnel entrance was Pyrious' box. Tonight, Pyrious had invited guests which meant Quinn as Pyrious's "trophy female" for the season was forced to sit on his lap as he and his cronies watched from the balcony. Why did Pyrious make her promise she would watch all of Luca's matches from his personal balcony? The sight of her, no matter where she was or what she was doing, always took Luca's breath away and simultaneously, the sight of them together made his blood boil.

"Keep it professional," Luca murmured. "We agreed. Strictly professional."

Could Pyrious have deeper plans than Quinn knew? Could Pyrious have something against him even though Quinn had promised to keep him safe?

Luca pulled his eyes from the sight as the announcer's voice came over the speaker again. "Connor the Courageous!"

Connor exited from the tunnel on the opposite side of the arena. He pointed at Luca, mimicking he was watching him then raising a fist at him. Without context, Luca assumed he was telling him this was his match and he was going to win. Luca just shook his head making the crowd grow louder at their public disagreement. As they watched one another from their respective sides, the announcer talked about the rounds.

This was the first round of three. By the end of three rounds, there would only be two men and two women left. These four would move up to the next competition. The next level of competition would start in two weeks as the other arenas finished their levels and the other set of competitors for this arena needed to have their rounds as well as a break.

Luca yawned. Everyone already knew how it worked but for some reason, the producer saw fit to remind them all every match. Maybe it helped to settle the nerves of the competitors to make the fights last longer. Eight matches for the women and eight matches for the men on the first round had to fill the entire day. People in the area of the arena could stay home from work and every Streamer was set to this arena. You couldn't escape it for three days.

The competitors took their cue as the announcer ended the intro to turn on their avatars and Luca turned on his glasses. He now saw and heard as if he was his avatar. Fighting this way took longer to get used to and he had worked hard to control his movements, but it was all still untested in the arena. Locating the centaur, he prepared for battle, holding his shield up in front of him, just under his eyes.

The centaur trotted back and forth in front of him until he was out of the periphery of the hawk's eyes.

Luca's avatar lumbered to turn and keep pace with the centaur, resulting in the centaur landing the first blow to Luca's side, sending him toppling to the ground, his shield and sword crashing loudly as they hit the wall where he had thrown them by accident as he tumbled.

Now the centaur reared up on its hind legs, and it grabbed the whip from its waist. With nothing to deflect the lashing, Luca was shocked repeatedly as his avatar took whip slashes. They were small shocks but in quick succession, causing him to drop to the ground from the pain. Rolling to one side, he was able to stand and stay facing the centaur who continued to lash at him from a distance. As his monstrosity recovered, Luca held up a hand, catching the end of the whip and yanking it toward himself with such force, he not only ripped it out of the centaur's hand but also brought the centaur to his front knees, hopefully giving Connor a painful shock to his legs.

Connor panicked, trying to recall the whip using the control piece in his hand but it couldn't come back to him. He holstered it again and tried to rise, but Luca took advantage of Connor's confusion to charge him. The legs carried his combination creature's full weight well, managing to get up to twenty miles per hour by the time he reached the centaur. A meaty arm ending with paw clothes-lined Connor's creature, flipping him head over feet. The centaur landed on its back, head crashing into the ground in such a way the audience groaned and gasped at the sight.

Clearly dazed, the centaur wrangled himself to his feet as Luca managed to slow down his avatar's heavy legs before he hit the wall of the arena. Luca managed to circle back around. The monster watched the centaur shake its head vigorously. Obviously, Connor received a shock to the head as he had done when he hit the ground, but it didn't appear to slow him down much. As Luca needed to recover from his sprint, the centaur charged him again. Instead of seeing the charge, Luca heard it first and began to pump his shoulders up and down, forcing his wings to flap, managing to get high enough. The centaur slowed but not in time to avoid receiving a slash in the chest from Luca's bear claws which was accompanied by another zap to Connor's bands.

Tilting to one side, wings still pumping, Luca managed to maneuver around Connor's avatar, but he was starting to realize the shoulder pumping was exhausting. Even if his avatar could keep up this pace, he couldn't and was forced to land in the middle of the arena floor. He tried to maneuver himself down by his sword and shield and was able to pick them up to resume a defensive position.

The voices of the crowd filled the arena as they shouted and cheered and gasped and jeered. Luca was certain he had followers, but he had to make this look like he wasn't sure how to fight while still managing to win. So far, he felt he'd done a good job of making himself look a little weak and slow, but he was unsure if it was enough to sway Pyrious to keep Quinn around.

Looking up to their balcony, Quinn gave him a thumbs up sign. He breathed in heavily at the reassurance but had taken his eyes off the centaur for too long. It had reared up again. Before he could react to the sounds, the centaur slammed into him again, shield colliding with sharp hooves, rolling Luca end over end across the arena. The pain from the shocks was almost too much to handle and Luca fell to the ground just like the avatar. The centaur had been taken aback by the blow but remained standing.

Cursing himself, Luca struggled to get to his feet. Why did he allow himself to get distracted? When he grunted, the mouth of the avatar released a weak growling sound, causing another round of laughter to echo throughout the arena. Finally, Luca made it to his feet but not before the centaur was already charging again. This time, Luca rolled to avoid Connor, lifted to all fours and maneuvered to grab his shield again, unsheathing the sword. Luca had heard through the chatter in the feed, that his ape having a sword in his hands was Connor's biggest fear. It clicked suddenly. Conner had been trying to prevent his avatar wielding the sword since the beginning of the match.

QUINN WATCHED IN HORROR as Luca struggled to rise. She remembered what that many shocks at once and all over had felt like. Pyrious slapped her on the knee for distracting him with her thumbs up. She had stolen Luca's attention away from the arena. If it cost him the match, Pyrious would be forced to pay out more than he would like. The long shot was still a lower pay out total than a Connor the Courageous win because people still didn't have confidence in Luca. But Pyrious wouldn't care and his temper could destroy her at any level of loss.

"Well, my dear, your plan is working splendidly. It doesn't seem to matter that he won. His avatar and his lack of skill are making him a less desirable bet, despite the option for big money. If he continues to win while looking this inept, you will make good on your word to make me a lot of money," Pyrious stroked her cheek and smirked.

Though she was surprised at Pyrious's optimism, his smile, no matter how facetious, always sent chills down her spine. She found him deplorable and hated having to be this close to him despite her word to the contrary. Once again, she wished she had been more careful. Hindsight was always clearer when you stared your future in its ugly face.

Luca rose to his feet. Quinn breathed a sigh in relief, but he wasn't safe yet. The centaur had moved in and was so close, it reared up and used its hooves to push on Luca's shield. Stumbling back, Luca lost the sword but not the shield. The centaur reared up for another run. Quinn covered her eyes as the crowd grew louder. Now at a deafening level of sound, she wouldn't be able to tell what was happening if she didn't look.

Instead of watching the avatar, she watched Luca. His breathing was labored from the many torso shocks he'd received. The strain showed on his face as he rolled and grabbed an invisible object with his hand. Then he pulled the prop that controlled the object on the field from his side, thrusting it forward. He looked silly, dancing around on the sidelines with no weapons. He lunged then ran in place. She could tell he'd stopped running because he did a balance check and lunged again with the prop.

The crowd 'Ooo'd' and 'Ahh'd,' gasping loudly after his latest lunge. Luca continued to move and dance, light on his feet only because of their training sessions. The first day, he had been clumsy and slow, thinking too much and not reacting fast enough but now, he was nimble and quick. She hoped his avatar was as nimble as he was, but she knew it would lag a little due to its enormous size.

Unable to take her eyes off him, she loved how he moved. Every concentrated muscle tensing and releasing to get his avatar to react accordingly. Pumping his shoulders reminded her of things she needed to forget but she couldn't. For a moment she was tempted to look at his avatar, to observe its wings at work. Then she realized how long she'd been watching Luca and not the match. She tore her eyes away to watch the avatar before Pyrious noticed. Her attention had been so diverted, she hadn't noticed Pyrious working his way up her bare thigh with his hand. Standing up, she went into the suite to visit the bar.

Safely behind the privacy glass, she watched the arena via the screen. Luca took a swing with his blade, barely missing the centaur. The crowd gasped again. Now, Luca wouldn't let the centaur get close or get behind him. He was becoming more accustomed to working the avatar and it was starting to show. But the centaur still had its advantages. The centaur turned, and its hind legs began kicking up dirt. The dust cloud grew bigger and bigger until Luca was forced to back up, and the first rows of the arena shielded their eyes and coughed, choking on the dusty air.

Unable to see or breathe, Quinn's face contorted into a look of fear and concern. Connor's tactic could end Luca if he couldn't find an answer. Luca's avatar's hands went up to his face as Quinn raced back to the balcony to see if she could see Luca. He'd covered his mouth with the neck of his shirt. His eyes were already shielded from the dust with his special goggles. The centaur began to charge in the monster's direction just as Luca began to pump his shoulders once again.

His act gave Quinn hope. If the centaur couldn't see any better in the dust, then he wouldn't know that Luca took off. A brilliant strategy. The head of the monster was now above the dust cloud as the crowd hushed in anticipation. When the centaur didn't make contact with the monster on the other side of the arena, he kicked up more dust and decided to check in another direction.

Luca and the spectators could see what Connor could not. As Luca's avatar hovered, he watched the centaur repeat the process over and over going in all directions blind to Luca's creature's location. Finally, Connor realized giant wings were pulling the dust upward, possibly hiding his opponent.

Luca acted. Using the currents in the dust, he swooped down toward the spot where the centaur should emerge this time, and picked up speed, raising the sword for a strike. Coming down, he located the centaur and swung the blade, half-blind. For a moment, neither reacted as the monster landed behind the centaur. Then, the centaur's head slid off its neck and Connor's avatar disappeared.

The crowd rose to their feet, erupting in a loud roaring cheer. Some people booed and jeered, claiming the fight was rigged. Luca's monster looked astonished as he rotated the blade from side to side. As the dust settled, Luca sheathed the sword and beat on his chest.

Quinn could imagine the historical images of apes made to beat their chests that would appear on Luca's feed, if they hadn't already.

Twenty-Three

"You need to look good for the victor's feast!" Sasha said, bringing a jacket into Luca's room. "They dropped off some options, but they left them in my room. It's the only one that looks remotely lived in." She smiled at his reflection in front of her. "You are very good at covering for us both, but you'll have to turn on the romance tonight."

Luca smiled back and knew he blushed a little, "I can't believe I managed to come out of the arena as a victor. The more I watch my replays, the more I realize I have no skill whatsoever and every time I win, it's really just luck."

"No, you're smarter than you give yourself creditor. You wouldn't be able to carry off the charade of having zero skills otherwise," she winked at him causing the redness to spread to his ears. "I've been paying attention."

"Well, I guess that makes you smarter than me," Luca said, choking down his embarrassment. "And a much better dresser." He turned to take in her gown. "So, am I supposed to propose to you this evening or just allude to a proposal. How do we want this to play out?"

"Considering I know the producers did everything to help me come through so we could move on together, I guess..." She bit her lip as she often did when she was trying to come up with a good lie, "I think you make allusions."

"Allusions it is," he said, taking her hand and twisting her around in one of the ballroom dance moves he'd spent last week learning.

"You are very light on your feet," Sasha giggled. "Shall we go?"

It was the first time either of them had been inside the Dome. Sasha had done her research explaining this was the entry hall everyone had to go through. The marble needed to be cleaned multiple times a day because this was actually where the electricity and water cars came in and out. So essentially, in reality they were in a street or a garage.

Luca stared at the pristine white marble and the towering columns. How could this place simply be a gateway? It was blocked off on the one side with a tall force field. When the field reset every few seconds, it shimmered in the moonlight. They weren't in the Dome exactly, but they'd made it to the entrance, which was just as exciting at this point in his life.

Off to one side was an enormous building made of black granite. The black against the white made for a startling and beautiful contrast. This building was as tall as the columns on the thoroughfare. A man at the entrance was ushering people inside it. Luca motioned and they followed the crowd after taking in the scale of this entrance.

"I didn't know people left the Dome," Sasha commented as they crossed the threshold of the black building. "But this is the detox center. You must burn your clothes and take a special shower. They've done it up nicely for us though. You usually come out the other side of the showers, where it's safe."

"Where do you get all this information?" Luca looked at her in amazement.

She fluttered her eyes at him, "I have my sources." She shrugged, "But that's why the drivers are separated and can't come out of the cars. You'll notice none of them do."

"A plethora of useless trivia." Luca chuckled.

"It won't be useless if we get to move here," Sasha sang in a high-pitched melody.

"You're too much." Luca said as he watched the sponsors come in from the shower rooms. "Will we have to change and burn these clothes?"

"No, we changed inside the arena, remember?" Sasha shook her head at him. "It's protected by a cleansing field. That way, the sponsors and dignitaries and producers can attend the battles."

"I never would have thought...I guess we're fine then." Luca said.

"I imagine we would have to take a special shower if we wanted to go further into the Dome though. We're just mostly not toxic. That's why everyone from the Dome is required to wear gloves."

Luca looked around the room, confirming everyone coming from the showers had on dressing gloves, "I guess that all makes sense on some level."

He watched as Pyrious entered with Quinn but tried to behave as if it didn't matter. Sasha tugged on his arm when she saw them, leaning her head in their direction. Clearly she was as tuned into them as he was.

She hissed, "We're together tonight, remember. It's important we keep up the act," she squared up to him pretending to fix his bow tie. "Let's take a pic for our feeds. Make sure we're trending because honestly, if it weren't for you, I never would have made it to the next round."

Luca groaned but put on a happy face and posed as they both raised their watches, "Capture," They said in unison. Within minutes, photos of them at the Victors Ball were rising in the ranks.

"So, trivia queen, who all attends this ball?" Luca asked as they did a turnabout the room.

"The victors from the western regions. All their fights are done," She motioned to a few other competitors in the room. "In two weeks, the southern regions will be done and then, we will start a round with all their victors. Then in about four weeks, we will move into the finals before the Dome."

"And what stream are the people in our region watching now?" Luca asked.

"The next round of exhibition matches of course," Sasha slapped his shoulder lightly and giggled at him again.

"They've already started another round?" Luca said incredulously.

"Of course. Remember, we had a week off?" She looked at him sternly. "That was so the next round could compete. And now, they have a week off while the next round of competition starts. You should know this. Don't you watch?"

"I have other things that keep me busy most of the time." Luca said.

"I forget how old you are sometimes. I don't think anyone your age has ever competed. In fact, I don't think anyone in their twenties has even come close to getting invited."

Luca grimaced at the comment. He hated knowing he was so much older than everyone. Looking at Sasha, he wasn't even sure how old she was and most of him didn't want to know. If she was too young, he would feel gross acting out this story line. Unfortunately, curiosity won out.

"How old are you? I just remembered. I never asked." Luca said.

"I'm 16." She replied casually.

His stomach turned. She wasn't even close to his age. "No wonder you think I am so old. You're barely out of school and haven't had to move into a specialty or anything." Luca replied.

"Thanks for reminding me that I am still just a child," She replied defiantly. "I'm old enough for the arena."

"But you kissed me," Luca was trying not to turn green.

"No offense, but please don't remind me. I'm just glad Quinn came in to talk to you about a sponsorship. I honestly thought she would convince you that first night. You've got a strong will, that's for sure. Most guys wouldn't last ten minutes with someone like her."

"Most guys can afford to be side-tracked," Luca quipped, looking at her, remembering her age. "Excuse me for a moment, dear," he feigned a smile and kissed her on the cheek, turning to head to the restroom.

He needed a moment to process and breathe. How was he supposed to pretend he was marrying a 16-year-old girl? How could he get out of this mess? Lost in his own mind as he walked, he barely noticed Quinn making a beeline for him. She bumped into him, grabbing his hand and pushing something into it. It didn't register there was a paper in his hand until he was staring at himself in the bathroom mirror.

Opening it, he noticed Quinn's handwriting was very nice. Perhaps she should have specialized instead of entering the arena. After reading it, he looked up. There was a steel door on the far side of the room. The note said she had already picked the lock, to go through it and follow the corridor to the end. Luca knew she was waiting but how long should he leave Sasha alone at the party? If Sasha ended up finding a sponsor like Pyrious... He couldn't stomach the thought.

He wished he could forget Sasha and her age and his age and the contract and competition and training, his head hurt just trying to process it all. With that, he checked the room, ensuring no one was watching, moved to the door, verified it was open and moved into the corridor, locking the door behind him.

Twenty-Four

As Luca reached the end of the corridor,Quinn was nowhere to be seen. His shoulders slumped. This was painful. Should he wait? How long?

Unable to decide, he threw his back up against a wall and slid to the floor, resting his head on his knees. The air down here was cooler than he thought it would be. Temptation surrounded him. He craved relief from his worries. Maybe he could hide in here for the rest of his life. That would make things less complicated but then Warren would have to fend for himself. If Warren was left alone, he wouldn't have the support he needed to specialize, and he would end up in the same position Luca found himself in now.

Tears began to stream down Luca's cheeks as he heard steps coming from down the hallway. He hadn't seen anyone, but he had passed plenty of heavy metal doors and hadn't checked a single one of them. Now he checked the one closest by his side, and it opened without difficulty. As the hinges squealed, he ducked inside, leavinga tiny slice open for him to see if he'd been followed.

Someone walked by and for a moment, Luca's eyes were blurry from the tears and he couldn't see clearly. He blinked and looked again. The person turning in circles and sighing in the hall was Quinn. She hadn't duped him. They hadn't much opportunity to talk since everything happened, even with her being able to visit him at night. Both agreed to focus on training, and all her tips went to good use. He had used every single tip she gave him in the arena. He got an idea and grinned. The hinges squealed as he opened the door a little more.

Quinn gasped and turned, "Who's there?" she asked,turning toward the echo and moving in his direction.

When she was close enough, he swung the door fully open, put his hand over her mouth and pulled her into the room. What he thought would be a funny joke turned ugly quickly as she threw him over the top of her and back into the hallway. Luca landed hard, flat on his back, knocking the wind out of his body.

He watched, dazed as she moved in to hit him and stopped. Her eyes grew wide.

"Luca!" she whispered tersely. "What in the world..."

Realizing he was hurt, she pulled him back into the room and closed the door. Quinn lit a lantern she found on the table. He'd not looked into the room when he'd entered it. As he focused on breathing, he looked around. On one side of the room was a small kitchenette, every inch of it covered in dust and grime.

Luca knew it hadn't been used in years. Quinn slid him to the other side of the room, where a bed, side table and dusty chair were glued into their stations. When he could breathe clearly, he sat up, his back resting against the bed.

"It's the old workers' camp. They dug tunnels down to minimize their exposure to the pollution while they were building the Dome. Now they work as service tunnels.

Most people don't even know these rooms are here." Quinn smiled. "Sorry, but you deserved it."

"I know," Luca coughed. Quinn dipped into her bag producing a flask. Breathing still hurt. He complained, "I don't think that's such a good idea right now."

He shifted and lifted himself off the floor and planted himself on the bed. A wave of dust flew up around them both. He coughed. Quinn sneezed, "It's water. When have you known me to drink but on a rare occasion?"

"I don't know. I only get to see you on rare occasions." Luca smiled at her.

"Take off your shirt, you jokester." Quinn commanded.

"Wow! That was quick. I'm not that easy you know." Luca feigned insult.

"I need to make sure I didn't break anything when I threw you. You can't go back to a party with fresh bruises and broken bones without people asking questions about where you've been."

"I see," he said as he took off his jacket and began unbuttoning his shirt. His pride helped him stifle the grimaces moving his torso caused. "So why exactly did you invite me down here then?"

"I wanted to spend some time alone with you. Like we used to when we were training. This was the perfect opportunity to leave the child out of our conversations," Quinn grimaced. She'd started grimacing whenever she mentioned Sasha back when he and Sasha had moved in together.

Luca wondered if he grimaced whenever he spoke of Pyrious. "Can we not discuss her right now? By the end of round two, I'm supposed to be engaged to a 16 year-old. It feels..." Luca sucked in his cheeks and shook his head.

"Like you're marrying a child?" Quinn finished. "You could say that" Luca looked at her, realizing he had no idea how old Quinn was either. What if she was almost as young as Sasha? Luca didn't know how long it had been since she was in the arena or how old she was when she went into the arena. He blanched.

"I know it might be a little late to ask but," Luca swallowed hard. "How old are you?"

"Relax. I'm twenty-one. There's only a few years between us." She smiled as she pressed against his abdomen. "Does that hurt?"

"Only because you're pushing on it," he chuckled. "It doesn't send shooting pains anywhere or anything. Not like being shocked."

She reached behind him, patting his shoulders and back. Luca could feel spots that would be bruised later but was able to not wince as she touched them. His ruse worked.

Quinn settled back and said, "Good. Then nothing appears to be broken, except maybe your ego," she winked at him.

He stood up quickly, wrapping his arms around her and pulling her down onto the dusty mattress, causing another haze of dust to kick up everywhere. Instead of getting closer, all they could do was cough in the thick air.

Coughing soon turned to laughter and laughter turned to embracing. Before they realized it, their lips were locked, feverishly fighting for attention and leverage.

Luca pulled away to catch his breath, "Is this what you had in mind?" His hands ran up and down her back, longing to remove her dress, any and all bruises forgotten.

As if reading his thoughts, she pulled away and stood up. Slowly, she unzipped the dress and let it fall to the floor. Luca's eyes followed every curve, every scar, every imperfection, drinking in her beauty before pulling her back to him for another round of touching and kissing.

Quinn pulled away again, "We can't be down here too much longer. Someone is bound to miss one of us soon."

"Really?" Luca leaned close. "Last I looked, Pyrious was getting drunk and hittingon all the young lady victors and Sasha was plowing into the champagne herself. No one will miss us for a while." He stopped to think, "How long have we been down here anyway?"

"Maybe thirty minutes or so," Quinn said, checking the watch she'd set on the side table without him noticing.

"Then we have plenty of time," Luca said, laying her down gently then standing to remove his pants.

As he crawled between her legs, he could tell when she felt him in just the right place. He worked her slowly, moving carefully and precisely until her eyes burst open and she gasped. This was her spot. She writhed beneath him, desperately wanting more. Luca worked himself in and out of her patiently until she screamed, and he felt her body clench to him and release, only allowing himself to finish after she was done. Exhausted, he flopped down beside her as she panted, still recovering from the explosion.

"Is that what it's supposed to feel like?" Quinn asked between breaths.

"If the person you're with is doing it right," Luca wore a proud smile.

"I thought you said you'd only had one serious relationship," Quinn looked at him quizzically. "So, where do you manage to develop those impressive skills."

"Just because I haven't had a lot of serious relationships doesn't mean I haven't had sex, Quinn. I thought I made that clear last time. Sometimes, you just need to work off some steam or take a break from the boredom," His smile faded a little as he saw the look on her face. She did not like his answer. "Now pull yourself together. We have a party to get back to."

He leaped over the top of her and sat down in the chair to put on his pants.

"Screw me and run huh?" Quinn sounded disgruntled. "Am I your break from the boredom or a release from the stress?"

"You're neither. I, uh, really want this to go somewhere. I, um, well, you're the one who said we needed to hurry and get back, but if you arranged for training this evening, I think I could arrange an encore," Luca's smile grew bigger and prouder as he spoke. He couldn't help it. He would never get used to having Quinn letting him love her that way 'just because.'

Twenty-Five

Quinn managed to get to the new Marcus meet up with time to spare. While Luca wasn't allowed to leave the arena dorms, she couldn't let that slow down her efforts for Pyrious. She had contractual responsibilities to make him so much money a month and while Luca had been more than enough, Pyrious was still holding her to the quota of med sales and other nefarious recruitment. The dark side of Quinn's life fell so much deeper than Pyrious vying for her intimate attentions. She needed to ruin as many lives as she could to stay on top of her agreement or there were penalties. While she waited for the new agreement to go into effect, she had to follow all the rules of the original one.

Tonight, she sat in the old warehouse. It was clear as she waited. Every night she hoped no one would show up looking for 'Marcus' but without fail, she was disappointed. If only the people on the outside knew all she knew. If only she could tell them. Right now, all she could do was hope to disrupt the flow of people by being covert and reporting the spot for activity over and over, shutting down this portion of the operation to no fault of her own. At least,that's what it looked like to her master and keeper.

She hadn't been at this spot for at least three weeks. Rai and Nallie had manned it while she was training with Luca but now he was into the second round, he needed her less and less. This worried her, especially considering his story line. Pyrious was making an appearance at his fights and others for the sake of running the bets and odds, but he took little pleasure in how much she immersed herself with Luca. Pyrious was starting to see she was too vested in Luca's successes and, tonight, he started asking questions she couldn't answer. To throw him off, she agreed to take some time away from him and sent Rai to train with Luca for the last few days. Rai reported Luca's disappointment but said he practiced the exercises and the video review went well.

The moon was full and gave the sky a burgundy hue against the pollution. She shook her head. Despite the toxicity, it was a beautiful sight. The concrete reflected the light, forcing her to adjust her lighting effects for people coming here to find her. Her watch ticked well past midnight before she heard the first steps. Her stomach dropped as they echoed in her direction. Taking her usual perch in the dark, she waited to see the face and evaluate the risk of her first prospect.

Her mouth dropped open and she audibly gasped when she saw the face. It was Warren.How had he found this place? Why was he here? There was no need for him to come here for anything. His brother was making it through the arena without issue. Did he know he could find her here? Before she could stop herself, she stepped out of the shadows.

"Warren?" she said. "What are you doing here?"

"Quinn?" Warren said. "What are you doing here?"

Quinn wanted to yell. She said, "I asked you first."

"Well, this seems very odd." Warren raised an eyebrow.

The look reminded her of Luca, which forced her to smile. Warren stared at her. From what she could see in his eyes, he was trying to work out what was going on. Suddenly his eyes opened wide and she knew he understood.

"You're Marcus?" he asked.

"How do you know about Marcus?" Quinn replied "Why do you answer every one of my questions with a question?" Warren whined.

"Because you still haven't answered any of my questions and I asked them first, "Quinn's tone was flat and even. "You really shouldn't be here."

A smirk crept across Warren's face. "He proposed to Sasha before her match today."

"I heard that was in the story line. Why do you think that matters to me?" Quinn replied coolly.

"You can't fool me. I know you and Luca like each other. I can see it written all over your faces when you're together." Warren shook his head. "He is in deep with you. Not like anything I've ever seen before."

"You've seen him with other women?" Quinn choked a little.

"Of course, I have. He's been raising me since our dad died. I was maybe two." Warren quipped. "I remember his only serious girlfriend, and she is no match for what he likes about you."

"I'm not sure that has any relevance as to why you're here," Quinn tried to wet her mouth. She hadn't realized it had gone dry. Her water bottle was in the desk. Moving toward it, Warren followed her.

"It has everything to do with why I'm here," Warren said, his tone laced with anger and frustration. "You weren't at the female matches today?"

"No," she sighed. "My keeper tends to send Rai to those. He's better with the ladies, if you know what I mean."

"I doubt you would've wanted to see it anyway. Probably would've upset you." Warren sounded sad more than frustrated at this point.

"You're probably right," she sat down at the desk, opening the drawer and taking a long drink. She offered him the bottle, but he waved it off.

"Quinn," Warren looked at her, his face suddenly full of fear. "He has to choose Quinn."

Quinn tilted her chin up, confused. "Who has to choose?"

"Luca." Warren choked a little. "He has to choose now."

"Choose what? What choices does anyone have in the arena?" Quinn quipped but as she saw the tears start streaming down his face, it dawned on her. "Sasha lost her match."

Earlier, when she heard his steps echoing up the stairs, she thought the pit in her stomach couldn't be buried any deeper. It wasn't a common reaction for her but now, she found she was wrong. The pit buried itself so hard, her entire core started to ache. As she watched him cry, the desperation of his situation was evident, and she knew why he was here.

"You need to find a way into the Dome yourself because Sasha lost and now he has to choose between his new fiancé and keeping up the charade or you, the one he did all this for."

"Makes for great drama, right?" Warren stammered through the tears. "They sent a car for me and everything. Sat me in the V.I.P. section. They told me it was because he was getting engaged and he wanted me there."

"There's nothing I know about your brother that makes that a lie," Quinn tried to soothe him.

He took a step back to keep her from touching him. "He proposed, and Sasha was so happy. They showed me on the screens as I cheered for them...for her. Then, she lost. They sent Luca out into the arena and then they showed us in a split screen."

"What did he do?" Quinn asked, raising a hand but Warren only took another tiny step back.

"Well, he was dumbstruck. He couldn't say a thing and the announcer said he was in shock and needed time. But you know the whole nation is watching. Waiting. For his decision and they won't let him move on before he makes it." The words tumbled out of his mouth faster than he could control them. "They took me to the dorms and to Luca and Sasha's rooms. They were just sitting there. She was bawling. He explained the only reason she'd made it this far was because the producers had managed to get her a pass. She was still fighting but she was always slated to win until this point." Warren shook his head. "Sasha started crying hysterically after he explained. Then she dropped to her knees, pleading with him. She couldn't go back home. Luca pushed her off him and looked and me before he...he just walked into his room and locked the door. I didn't know what to do or say. So, I left."

"And now you're here, looking for Marcus."

"I didn't realize that would be you but I'm kinda glad it is. How else would I explain all this to someone else?" Warren dropped to the concrete floor, curling up into a ball, his head tucked into his chest and his hands holding his ankles. "When someone comes here, you have to be strong. Show no weakness. Weakness is bad for negotiation."

"So is desperation," Quinn said. "Which is what your brother came to me with in the first place." She gave Warren a weak smile as she moved to sit next to him. "That's something hard to hide from someone like me. I see right through most people."

"I think that's why Luca likes you so much. You don't bull shit him and he can't bull shit you." Warren's voice was muffled as he laid his cheek on his knees. "Well, that and...I imagine you know what you look like. Most of the pretty girls in our block won't give him the time of day because he didn't specialize but I imagine you knew that."

"Beauty is in the eye of the beholder. Plenty of those pretty girls scoffed at me when I came to visit you guys."

"Still doesn't solve my problem," Warren sniffled. "You know Luca will pick you," she shook his arm a little. "You have to know that."

"Do I? Will he? Look at the situation, Quinn. He just proposed to her. Just pledged to spend the rest of his life with her. If he abandons her now, he loses favor with the public and looks like a complete ass. If that happens, he will be voted out by the producers, and you know they can rig anything." Warren tried to choke back more tears.

Quinn went quiet, taking in everything Warren said. On one hand, he was right but on the other, the public might be just as likely to hate him for abandoning his little brother for a girl he barely knew. Of course, with the way the producers had played up the story line between them, others might not see them as mere acquaintances. Running the scenarios through her head, she realized what the producers were trying to do. He was costing them too much money in the legit gambling circuit, and they'd been instructed to cut him out before finals. That would be the only explanation for why they'd pushed the proposal in round two instead of round three. She swallowed hard.

"On one hand, you may be right, but the public might hate him just the same for abandoning you." Quinn said.

"I thought of that," Warren said. "And the more I thought about it, the more I realized I had to come here because Marcus could do for me what he did for Luca. He could get me in the next local round, which starts next week. Then it's not like he's abandoning me because he knew I was in. It's the only way the producers will let him stay."

"I didn't even know people from outside knew about the producers," Quinn lamented.

"I didn't until tonight," Warren lifted his head and sat up, giving her a weak grin. "It's the only way this can happen for both of us." He leaned into her, shoving her lightly.

She laughed and shoved him back. At least now someone knew her struggle and she felt like someone may be in this with her for the first time since she met Luca. It was a no-win situation for all of them. Thinking about every avenue, she had to come up with a solution, a plan. Pausing, she stood up, pulling Warren up with her.

He stood defiantly, "So are you going to help me or not?"

"I think I may have a way out of this. One Luca won't freak out about and one my master may just buy into. Give me until tomorrow night. Okay, Warren? Tomorrow night."

Twenty-Six

It was nearly dawn by the time Quinn managed to get to the competitor dorms. She wasn't certain if either of them would answer considering the circumstances. When Sasha appeared at the door, Quinn jumped. Inside, Quinn tried to sit them all in the same room, but it was apparent Sasha and Luca were arguing over the decision. When Luca finally came out, Sasha retreated to her room and slammed the door.

"So, you've made a decision?" Quinn asked.

"Is that what this all sounds like?" Luca asked. "This is because I refuse to make a decision yet."

"You know they will ask you in the interview after your match. If they have any indication you're not choosing her, you'll probably be out too, regardless of your skills."

"You think I don't know what happens if I fall out of favor with the producers or the public?" Luca began pacing around the room erratically. "If I stay with her, the public buys the love story, and my numbers stay up but not as high as before because that would mean I would abandon my brother. If I don't choose her, the producers guarantee my vilification. He asks a girl to marry him then takes it back when he has to choose between her and his little brother. What ever happened to true love winning out?" He stopped to look at Quinn, trying to control his tone. "My numbers may not drop that much but the producers would rig it for ruining their drama, but the people would see me being a loyal brother. Well, until the inevitable spin. This is...I don't know what to do, Quinn. Either way, it probably ruins my chances for the final round."

Quinn motioned for him to sit down and for longer than Luca or Quinn felt comfortable, they both stayed silent. Quinn felt the energy in the room needed to calm down and Luca was just exhausted and tired of talking about his horrible choice. As the silence lingered, the bedroom door opened. Sasha slumped down on the couch, opposite Quinn and released a long, loud breath.

"I am assuming you came because you may have a plan," Sasha said without much enthusiasm, looking at Quinn intently.

"Well," Quinn bit her lip. It was less of a plan and more like a strategy but some of the details were more than she could ever ask from anyone. "It's more of a plan of action maybe. But there are parts none of us will like."

"What is it?" Luca looked at her.

She knew he was desperate for a solution to problem. This was the worst possible plan for the consequences.

"Well, we can get Warren on the list for the arena rounds that start next week," Quinn started with the easiest information to relay.

Luca shot to his feet, "Absolutely not! I will not allow him to be subjected to the shocks and the producing and the crazy. He's too young..."

Quinn raised a hand without looking at him, "He won't go past the exhibition. We'll find a way to remove him from the competition before the first round actually starts."

"What? How?" Luca stopped moving, shocked and stressed into silence. After a few deep breaths, he said, "I still won't allow it. I am his guardian and I say no."

"According to the rules, he doesn't need your permission, Luca." Quinn rose to her feet. "You know this. Besides, if you don't allow it, he'll find another way, which will put him in harm's way for sure."

"How would you know what he would do? Seriously, Quinn. You think you can read anyone," Luca began pointing at her angrily. "He knows specializing is his best option. He's specializing in..."

"He came to find Marcus last night." Quinn said, stopping Luca in his train of thought.

He looked dumbfounded again, "What..."

"He came to the warehouse last night looking for Marcus to get him into the arena. Going with his plan was the safest idea I could muster up in such a short period of time. The producer will love the idea of you going back to train with your little brother. It buys us all a little more time to figure a way out of this mess. He'll only fight in the exhibition and then the producer swill find some way for him to leave the competition. It broadens your story." Quinn explained.

"What if they can't find a way to get him out of the competition?" Luca looked at her imploringly.

"That's the least of our issues," Quinn said, moving in closer to Luca, putting her hands on his chest. He pulled away. "There's so much more than that and the rest is worse."

"How could it be worse?" Luca plopped back down into the chair.

"Well, the whole choice thing is the producer's way of thinning you out. It gives them a reason not to allow you on to the third round, no matter what you choose. If we pull off this thing with Warren, you would move into the third round and buy Sasha more time. It makes the issue a non-choice until it's absolutely necessary."

"I'm still waiting for the parts that are worse," Luca said.

"So am I." Sasha mumbled. "So far, this is sounding not so bad."

"The bad part is that I have to ask Pyrious for the favor to fix it for Warren and I have to convince him it was worth his time to do this for all of you. He will be willing, but there will be costs."

"We have Digicreds," Sasha smiled. "That doesn't sound so bad."

Luca locked eyes with Quinn. Quinn could see he knew she was mortified by the price and had a few guesses as to what it could possibly be.

"She doesn't mean creds, Sasha,"Luca said, refusing to break the link with Quinn. Quinn swallowed hard enough that it echoed around the room.

"I don't understand, Luca. How could there be a cost if she's not talking about creds? Things cost creds."Sasha asked innocently.

Luca broke his trance and shook his head, moving to the couch next to Sasha.

Quinn's look moved directly to the floor. "Naïve child," she mumbled as she made her lip bleed piercing it with her teeth.

"I am not naïve," Sasha snorted as she proceeded to pout.

"Yes, you are, because you don't see the costs of living in this world. Being in the Dome means you have to make sacrifices." Quinn hissed.

"No. Quinn? Did you have to..." Luca stood up again and moved toward Quinn, trying to comfort her. "Oh my God, Quinn. Tell me I'm wrong."

"I haven't had to do anything yet. It's not me I'm worried about." Quinn looked at Sasha. The look on her face was anguished.

Luca gasped, "Oh, Quinn. No. You can't be serious." He looked from one female to the other, torn between which he should feel more sorrow.

"I don't understand," Sasha eyed both like a wide-eyed deer. "What are you not telling me?"

"Sasha, this course of action is unacceptable. I won't agree to it. I won't agree," Luca said, shaking his head furiously.

"Luca, I don't understand. You have to explain."

"Sasha, Pyrious has asked..." Quinn started.

"No, Quinn. You can't ask her to do that. Even if it would save us all. You can't ask her." Luca protested, physically moving his body between her and Sasha in as if he was an obstacle.

"Ask me to do what?" Sasha asked. "What do I need to do in order to help all of us?"

"No, Sasha. It's not a good choice and you should never have to make it," Luca turned to Sasha, his look desperate for her to listen.

"I have a right to know what my options are, Luca, even if you don't like them." Sasha said. "I came to the arena to give me more options to live and not even you will take away my choices."

"You cannot sign a contract with Pyrious as your sponsor. It is absolutely out of the question." Luca demanded.

"It's not a contract, Luca." Quinn said calmly. "Well, I guess it could be a contract but..." Quinn shook her head then rested her forehead in her hands.

"What do you mean it's not a contract?" Luca turned to Quinn.

"What's a contract?" Sasha asked but Luca waved her off.

"What's the deal, Quinn?" Luca pressed.

"She has a choice. When Pyrious insisted she sign a sponsor contract, I told him that would never happen. That you wouldn't allow it to happen as you weren't very fond of him. So, he gave her a choice. A contract or...one night. Before he'll go to the producers he has in his pocket for a deal, he wants a contract from one of you and a night with her. The night with her is non-negotiable."

"Quinn! How could you ever think this would be a presentable idea?" Luca covered his mouth, his eyes wide.

"Would someone explain my choices to me?" Sasha chimed in.

"I figured it might be more manageable if she only had to give up one night instead of a life of indentured servitude," Quinn said defiantly.

"Okay, so what would happen on this night?" Sasha stood up. "I have a right to know."

They both turned and looked her up and down. Luca shook his head. Quinn looked horror-stricken as the look of anguish returned to Sasha's face. Then, her eyes flickered to the bedroom door. Sasha rose off the couch, following her gaze.

"Really. You mean he wants..." she went pale for a moment. "That's the price? That's what you meant as payment?"

"I already told you, Sasha. We'll find another way," Luca insisted.

"It's not like I'm a virgin, Luca. This isn't something I'm not familiar with. But he's just so..." Sasha's face puckered and distorted into something unattractive. "He's so old."

It was Luca's turn to look dumbfounded, "You've done that before."

"Oh please. Welcome to the modern world. If I don't make it into the Dome, I'll be lucky to make it past the age of 40. My life is almost half over. It's not like any of us have time to waste," she put her hands on her hips and snorted defiantly. "Well, except maybe Quinn because she lives in the Dome now." She huffed and sat back down. "So, I get a free ride to the Dome if I sleep with some old guy." Looking thoughtful, "I suppose it can't hurt. When will he be here?"

For a moment, Quinn was too shocked to speak, and Luca had started mumbling incoherently to himself.

Quinn recovered first, "Pyrious isn't just some old guy. He's not nice, Sasha. He won't be nice."

"What do you mean?" Sasha asked.

"He's not nice in regard to your...um...body or well...anything really. He may hurt you and he won't care if you tell him to stop." Quinn said.

"But I do this, and I make it into the Dome, right?" Sasha said.

"I can't believe either one of you is considering this a viable option," Luca said loudly.

"I don't really see us having any other choice. He only gave us an hour to decide," Quinn said.

"I've had to do worse things to get what I need," Sasha said. "What? Don't tell me you guys thought I was that innocent."

"I don't even know what to think about you right now," Luca waved her off again. "But I guess, if you're fine with it..." He shook his head and headed to the kitchen. Quinn figured the entire discussion had made his throat dry. Hers sure was. Then he turned back to her half-filled glass in hand, "Wait! Didn't you say something about a contract, Quinn?"

She'd been hoping he'd not notice. "Yes, I did. But that will be resolved too," Was it the pain in her eyes that made it impossible for Luca to look away?

He yelled, "What? Quinn!" the glass fell into the sink, shattering against the metal and spraying water upward. Luca shielded his face, but some shrapnel found its way into his hands and arms. Quinn ran to the kitchen, grabbing a rag and yelling for Sasha to bring tweezers.

Quinn pulled him to the counter and began to remove the shards as he winced. Then she stopped the bleeding, swabbing each wound. He touched her face, smearing blood on her cheek.

"I held him off for as long as I could, but I just couldn't let him trap either one of you." Quinn could not halt the tears that fell from her eyes.

Twenty-Seven

As he walked into the arena, Luca was numb. So numb, he didn't really notice the battle shocks or when he won the round or when he interviewed with one of the producers and chose Sasha over his brother. He'd certainly rehearsed his words sufficiently.

Directly after the live interview, they played the list of new invites with pictures and he watched as Warren's face splayed across the screen, but he still didn't react. His entire plan was spiraling out of his control. Now he wouldn't be able to be with Quinn, and his brother would take Sasha's place. Worse, Sasha was just a kid. How could he just abandon her like that?

He knew getting a repeat invite was nearly impossible. Maybe once he worked his way up the ranks he could invite her inside as a consolation prize, but he wasn't sure how long that might take. Would he get kicked out once he was welcomed in? All these questions and no answers kept his head swirling well through the next few days. Suddenly, he realized he was at the national arena, one round from the finals in the Dome. Sasha was with him and Warren was on the screen in an exhibition match.

The first phase of Quinn's plan had actually worked. They had managed to buy the time they needed. But was it enough to keep favor with the public? Once they found out Warren was expelled from the matches, wasn't Luca responsible for making the decision again? All he knew is he didn't want to choose between two kids and he wanted Quinn back. She promised to return for training and watching his last set of matches, but she would have been with that awful man in the meantime. He couldn't stomach the thought of it all.

Could he dare hope it would work? Every single thing they had rigged in the hopes none of it exploded in their faces. They were most likely okay, but...Luca shook his head. He couldn't face any of it. He pushed all the thoughts from his mind.

He clinked glasses with yet another stranger trying to talk him up at the welcome party. He'd learned to detest parties. Too many of them and for everything. The excess and overwhelming opulence and what Luca assumed, the waste. Food and drink and goods alike. The Dome's party budget could probably feed his Bloc for years.

Quinn told him this was the normal social life inside the glass walls, but at the time, he doubted they celebrated all accomplishments with a party. Now he believed her because they forced him to be at every one of these pointless events, showing him off like something precious and rare, something to be bought and sold. And maybe that was the point. Every contestant was for sale, in a manner of speaking. Sasha never saw this side of things, and she was still mostly oblivious. Luca noticed it right away, possibly due to his education from Quinn before he received his invite.

After the party, Luca drifted back to his quarters. There, he sunk into the emotional shock again and blacked out for at least another day. Rolling through the motions and doing as he was told, he barely acknowledged anything around him. His interviews were subpar, and his following was suffering but he never noticed. The more entrenched in this world he became, the worse he felt about this entire situation.

Before this all began, he thought he lived in desperation. At this moment, he was more desperate than he ever felt before the arena. All his work had done only increased his level of disparity and reminded him of all the things he might never have. As he prepared himself to face the final rounds, he finally understood the purpose of the arena.

He knew now his entire life was never actually in his control. It had been orchestrated by someone else since his birth. Choices didn't exist here. When he thought about it too much, it made him even more numb. He was actually paralyzed in this moment; he couldn't break free from the hopelessness he felt.

From the bathroom, he heard a knock on his bedroom door. Only three people knew he stayed in a separate room within Sasha's and his quarters or at least three people he was sure about. He couldn't tell what the producers did or did not know. For a minute, he felt elated as he jaunted toward the door with a smile on his face. When he opened it, he found Sasha on the other side. His shoulders slumped, and he retreated into his sitting area. The rooms were bigger and fancier as he worked through the levels.

"I know I'm not the one you desperately want to see. I just wanted to say thank you. If you want, we can stage some monumental break-up at the party tonight," Sasha smiled at him in the way she always did, with compassion and concern hidden by supposed innocence and true self-indulgence.

"It's not that. I just, I am..." he released a heavy breath. "I've got a lot on my mind."

"I've noticed. You hardly say or do anything anymore," she approached him cautiously. "Luca, your following is dropping. If you don't snap out of this, you will not make it to the final round in the Dome. Everything you fought for, schemed for. All of it will be for nothing. Warren will never survive the arena, at least not in one piece. The deal is contingent upon you making it to the Dome."

"What party is tonight?" Luca asked, flopping down in his chair.

"The Final Victor's party. It's for sponsorship. I know you don't want a sponsorship, but they insist we go and make an appearance as the star couple. We must be seen to keep your story line going," Sasha sighed as if exhausted by the entire process.

"Keeping up appearances," Luca grumbled. "If you stage a break-up, they'll send you home."

"But our story line is so hot, thanks in large part to you. Well, and the rumors of our disappearances at events circulating through the producer's offices. Everyone is so enamored and intrigued by our story, I may be the first in a long time to get a second invite. If not for any other reason but to mend my broken heart from my tumultuous affair in the arenas," she faked a painful glance at him, which forced him to smile.

"You should specialize in producing. As well as you can act, you would be an interviewing producer in no time," Luca threw his pillow at her, knocking her off balance and onto the bed. His face strained with concern, "Sorry. Didn't mean to throw it that hard. Never would have been able to before."

"I know. I'm just glad I was close to the bed," she laughed as she tossed the pillow back to him. "I'd like to think, if I met you in different circumstances. Maybe we would've been able to make this work. You're a pretty decent guy, not like that Pyrious dude." Luca winced at the name. "Sorry, I know he's a sour subject for you."

"What happened when he wanted, well...you know?" Luca asked softly.

"Well, he came in and said we were going to get down but then Quinn left, and he just sat in the chair and drank. He watched me prance around but never tried anything," her mood became sullen. "It appears everyone in my world wants Quinn and not me." She fought back a few tears. "It's not that I wanted him to do something, you know. It would just be nice to not be second to her. Here, I'm not important to anyone unless I'm seen on your arm and that's all you want from me because of her too. I can't even talk you out of this room, even when I do it just so your numbers can go up and you can stay."

"Would it make you happy if you got to choose everything for a day?" Luca asked, correcting quickly, "Within the boundaries of my comfort levels, of course."

Sasha smiled again, "Is there something wrong with me?"

"No, of course not, Sasha. You're just...too young for me. I don't feel comfortable exploring a relationship like that because I am so much older than you are. It feels wrong to me," he explained.

"I suppose we could have a day of fun. It would provide lots of photo ops and get the producers off our backs for story line for once," Sasha reasoned, Luca assumed it was more for her than for him.

The twinkle returned to her eyes as she convinced herself this was an excellent plan. Racing to his closet, she grabbed a shirt and flung it at him. "Get dressed. If this is our last few weeks on this free ride. We're going to live it up today."

Suddenly regretting the suggestion, he put on the shirt with a grimace. She grabbed his hand and dragged him out of the dormitories so fast Luca found himself tripping over his own feet trying to keep up with her pace. They both laughed as they watched the camera man and producer stumble after them as well. There was a small part of Luca hoping they would manage to elude the camera due to their inability to film at Sasha's pace, but he would not be so lucky.

The producers followed Sasha and Luca as they explored the new area. There were weird falls of bubbly water and a small museum with stuffed carcasses of native animals that used to roam this region.

Luca's favorite was the old school movie playhouse showing something called films on a large screen with soft chairs for the audience to lounge in as they watched. It was his first time seeing something called cartoons and he found the crazy characters delightful, wishing they had something like this in his Block, promising himself he would show Warren. This area must be ranked higher than theirs as they were only permitted to view the feed.

As they went from place to place, people stopped them, asking for Luca's autograph. More than once, he and Sasha tried to 'sneak away' to share private kisses but the cameras always found them quickly. All of it fed into the producers' story of the lovebirds wanting to be private about their affair. Thwarting them was the cameraman's job, but at least they made it easy, and they were often thanked by the crew for it. Luca knew now if the crew lost them, they would probably lose their jobs.

After seeing the local sights, Sasha called a car and they went back to visit Warren at the arena. Together they helped him train and talked in the privacy of Waren's room, just as Luca had done earlier in the week. This time, they both taught Sasha some defensive moves. Luca was certain they were on the feed all day and all night. Tomorrow,they wouldn't have warranted so much attention as the exhibition matches for their original block were premiering. Warren would be on the national feed in two nights' time, and they assured him they would both be in attendance to show support.

Luca was exhausted as they raced back to their room for some 'privacy' before dinner. As the door flung open and they walked in, they froze at the sight.

"Did you leave the lights on?" Sasha asked, eyes darting around the room.

"No, did you?" Luca responded in the same fashion.

"You're both right. Neither of you left the lighton," the voice came from the corner with the kitchen. "I thought after such a day, you would both enjoy a home cooked meal."

Luca recognized the voice where Sasha didn't. His eyes confirmed it was Rai. Nallie was with him, chopping away at something green he'd never seen before.

"I thought Quinn was coming for training," Sasha said innocently.

"She sends her regrets," Rai frowned. "But she is otherwise...engaged."

Luca swallowed the lump forming in his throat, but his stomach ached over the idea.

"Otherwise engaged?" Sasha asked.

"Yes, she's at a special dinner with Pyrious," Nallie frowned. "It was supposed to be our dinner but, well, sometimes even the best laid plans."

Luca felt his face go livid as his grip tightened on Sasha's hand. She winced and shook free, "We're not out anymore. No need to pretend," she scowled at him, shaking her hand.

He didn't notice Sasha's glare. Focused on staying calm so they couldn't report him for treason, they continued to stand with the door open. A camera peered in, hoping to catch a glimpse of the private quarters of the best love story every written for the show. Rai grimaced and growled, stomping toward the door, slamming it shut.

Only when the door clamored and echoed throughout the room did Luca break out of his trance. Shaking his head, he watched Rai return to the kitchen. His mouth was suddenly dry, and he needed to punch something.

"Don't worry. She managed to secure some sleeping pills from the doc. He has taken a shine to her over the years," Rai smirked at Luca. "She's been slipping them into Pyrious' drink, and he hasn't been able to...well, I guess you can imagine the rest."

The look on Luca's face turned from anger to horror as he tried to wipe away the images Rai put there on purpose; then to shock at the idea Rai knew what he was thinking.

"Don't worry. Your secret is safe with me. The last thing any of us needs is an investigation in the house of Pyrious," Rai smiled slyly. "Besides, she's in no mood to see you. She's been watching the feed all day."

"Oh," Luca said, looking at Sasha then back to Rai. "She said she never watches the feed."

"How could she resist? You two are so cute together. I'm hoping to catch a kiss before we leave," Nallie grinned at them both.

"Nallie dear, we shouldn't bother them right now.

Let's make dinner while they retire to their room for some much-needed privacy," Rai said, nodding toward Sasha's door. "We'll stay in the second bedroom."

"Ummm," Luca started.

"No worries. I've already swept it while Nallie was cooing over the décor. She loves what you've done with the place. Nothing to worry about."

"Is she really that..." Luca began again.

Rai interrupted, "Yes, she is that sweet. Our Nallie is the sweetest woman you'll meet but sometimes, she only sees or hears what she wants," he nodded again toward the door. "Go on now. I am sure you'll want a nap. Being on feed all day can be exhausting, I'm sure."

Twenty-Eight

The crowd chanted and cheered as Luca entered the field. For the first time, arena play felt different. This field wasn't dirt. It had grass and bushes, like a natural obstacle course. Maneuvering might prove to be difficult. He had learned earlier this arena changed based on the producers' wants and needs for excitement. Obviously, they evaluated the weaknesses in his avatar and inserted bushes and trees, so he would be at a disadvantage against his nimble opponent, solidifying everyone's assumptions the producers were trying to cut him before the final rounds. He began to think they shouldn't have taken the power by circumventing the producers' last attempt to thwart him.

Regardless, production games were the last thing on his mind. As he walked in, he saw Quinn, sitting on Pyrious' lap, a wide grin on Pyrious' face. The fire burned through his face as he watched her feed him grapes and run her hands through his hair.

"She looks to be enjoying herself," he mumbled.

They hadn't spent but a few seconds together since the night Quinn gave him and Sasha the plan. Making herself scarce even at the parties, she managed to keep him at quite a distance, distance he needed to keep him from attacking Pyrious in the first place. He doubted Pyrious allowed her a long leash. He focused on the plan. If he won, he would return to the dorms and play card games with Rai until dawn before being forced to pack. At the end of the week, he would move into the Dome, and Warren would become too ill to fight.

Glaring at the balcony, he didn't hear the announcements. The match started without him noticing. Quinn gave him a look of concern as the nimble knight, the announcer's name for the other avatar, tackled him, sending both avatars rolling onto the ground and flinging his shield and sword across the arena floor. Luca wasn't fast enough to get to the knight with the obstacles. This avatar successfully disarmed him within seconds because of the bushes and trees but mostly because he allowed himself to be sidetracked by Quinn.

"Keep it professional," he whispered, not that his voice could be heard over the crowd.

He heard Sasha, screaming her support, she was no doubt horrified by his work, but it did little to help the situation as the knight tried to remove his avatar's head gear. Luca struggled against the knight's strength and persistence, bashing on the metal armor with his fists. If the knight managed to remove his creature's helmet, Luca would be done. It would probably be the quickest match in national arena history.

Suddenly, the knight switched moves, throttling him as hard as he could. Luca was being shocked in the neck so much he could barely breathe. These shocks felt stronger than the ones in earlier rounds. Or was it the location because the knight managed to get close? He couldn't be sure, but he focused on his breathing and how to get out of the knight's grasp.

Luca clapped his hands against the sides of the knight's head. They clanged off the helmet, causing the knight to stop. The vibration should ring through the knight's ears and Luca assumed it stunned him. Either way, it was a diversion lasting long enough for Luca to get a good hold on him. Using all the strength he could muster, Luca pushed the knight as hard as he could, which was harder than he thought because the knight went sailing through the air and landed in a nearby bush. Wheezing, Luca rolled the avatar to its feet and turned to face the knight, but he had disappeared.

Not willing to go searching, Luca looked around, ears finely tuned to the clanking sound of armor as he did. Seeing his shield and sword on the other side of the arena floor, he contemplated moving toward it. In earlier matches,he was adamant about keeping his hands on his accessories. Maybe that was it. The knight was probably expecting him to go for his sword and shield during the moment of reprieve and freedom. If the knight watched any of the stream like Luca did, he would be set up for a surprise attack there. Luca couldn't bear the idea getting shocked again after the throttling. He changed tactics.

When he looked around, he scrutinized the trees. There was one a few steps away and it would give him a decent vantage point to see if he could spot the knight. The crowd fell silent as they watched him climb. He reached the bottom branches and looked up to find another hand hold when his enhanced vision saw something glint off the lights. It was the knight with its back to him, facing the sword and shield, bow poised to fire.

No wonder the crowd went silent. They watched him climb this tree. Luca wouldn't have taken his eyes off him if he'd been the one in the tree. One of Quinn's first lessons was to never turn his back to anyone, in combat or in life. You never know where an opponent might turn up. He now knew this advice was for this level of competition because all the other arenas were wide open with nowhere to hide.

Trying not to rustle any leaves, he moved in as close as he could. It was becoming obvious the knight couldn't hear much through the helmet, but Luca wasn't sure if it was because he had boxed the knight's ears or if the helmet was designed that way to muffle the noise of the crowd. The knight looked up. Luca froze. If he got his shot off this close, Luca was out for certain. The crowd gasped collectively, watching the tree intently. The knight looked back at his target, then down to the ground before settling himself in a little longer. Without a look over his shoulder, the knight pivoted and turned around.

Luca stared at the point of the arrow as it sat inches from his eyes. Instinctively, he grabbed it with his hand just as the knight released the string. The lack of movement caused the bowstring to snap; the sound echoing over the quiet crowd as they gasped again. Ripping the bow out of the knight's hands, Luca threw it to the ground. Without checking for support, Luca rolled onto his back and smashed his feet into the knight's chest with all his might. The knight flew out of the tree as Luca tumbled backward, ripping his wings on the branches, making them useless. Feeling himself falling, he tried to control it, grabbing at branches and the trunk itself as he tumbled out of the tree.

Hitting the ground hard, Luca was shocked all over by the impact, knocking the wind out of him and blinding him temporarily. Forcing his lungs to move, he shook off the blurry vision from the tears and scoured the arena. The crowd erupted, jumping to their feet and Luca thought he heard the announcer's voice. His ears were hearing a menacing echo with every word made worse by the crowd. He grabbed his head and thought he recognized Sasha's face before his world went fuzzy and then dark.

Twenty-Nine

Luca blinked his eyes into focus. He laid flat on something soft and surrounded by a sea of white. A high pitched ringing pierced his ears. His wrist and hand felt constrained and there was a chill on his cheeks. The air smelled fresh, but his lungs hurt with each breath. Every muscle in his body ached and a few organs did too.

Looking down, he saw someone holding his hand. It wasn't Quinn so he guessed it was Sasha before he followed the arm up to the face. Sasha smiled at him. Her eyes were puffy from tears.

Maybe she wasn't just using him to make it into the Dome after all. She had said she would stage a break-up after the final match. Luca knew she wouldn't be able to complete or keep that promise now. It would make her look like a cold; heartless person and she wanted a shot at being invited to the arena again. Her sponsor was already pitching it to the producers, but he wasn't sure how he knew that. Had she told him that before? No, but she had alluded to it. Who was her sponsor? He'd forgotten to ask.

Apparently, they didn't have as much pull as Pyrious did because it was taking weeks to get this story line done. The producers hadn't agreed to it if he remembered right after eavesdropping on some of their conversations.

How long ago was that? How long had he been in this room? Luca tried desperately to remember anything after the knight went flying out of the tree, but he couldn't. Groaning, he tried to turn his head. Sasha released his hand and he saw her stand up abruptly, her lips moving but he couldn't hear anything, just a constant buzzing sound.

It didn't make sense. Luca could hear the sensors beeping. Maybe he could only pick up certain frequencies now. Watching Sasha move to the door and motion to others outside, he expected it to be the producers to give them the low down on their next moves. He watched as Rai, Nallie, Warren and Quinn entered the room. This was a brazen visit and one he probably would have only received if he had lost.

Sasha came back in, grabbing his hand. Her face was excited and her lips were moving but he still couldn't hear her voice. Scrunching his eyes, he tried to make his ears work to no avail. Releasing a long, heavy sigh, they all looked at him. Luca had released a groan without realizing it or hearing it.

Rai and Nallie hung near the end of the bed, watching the door carefully, each periodically pacing around the room. Quinn came to the other side of him, grabbing his other hand and caressing his face. As her lips moved, he couldn't hear her either. Opening his mouth to speak, nothing came out or at least he thought nothing came out. He tried to say he couldn't hear but his mouth was so dry, he was almost certain all he managed to do was choke and chortle. Without missing a beat, Sasha exited the room and returned with a glass full of water, helping him drink it as she and Quinn exchanged glances. When he was done and the cotton mouth was gone, he tried again.

Although he couldn't hear his own voice or feel it coming out of his throat, whatever came out of his mouth caused the room to erupt. Sasha returned to the door.

Quinn actually shed a few tears and Rai just looked at him, eyes wide but compassion on his face. Nallie just threw her arms up limply and sat down in the chair, searching the side table for the remote.

Doctors came rushing into the room, their mouths moving. It was no use. His ears were broken. A nurse came in with a board and marker. She scribbled on it feverishly then turned it to face Luca.

"Can you hear the doctor?" Luca read.

He shook his head causing pain to shoot from his shoulders up over the top of his brain and landing on his forehead, square between the eyes. Grabbing at his head, he winced and probably groaned again but he couldn't tell. The nurse erased the bored and took to writing as quickly as possible again.

"Can you tell when you are speaking or making sounds?" He read, again shaking his head, forced back down by the pain.

The nurse flipped the board again and he squinted to read the smaller lettering. "Is there anything you remember hearing or can hear right now?"

He pointed to the machines beeping in the corner.

Maybe he couldn't hear them beep as much as sense them, inserting the beeping sound in his mind. He felt his lips moving and maybe he relayed this thought, but he couldn't be sure. Becoming more frustrated by the moment, the nurse looked at the doctor. Both looked stricken, as if they'd heard something horrible. The doctor shook his head and looked at Luca, then Sasha, motioning for her to join him outside. Luca motioned for Quinn to go with them. He tried to say she should know too. The nurse prompted Quinn to join Sasha and the doctor.

"How long have I been here?" Luca said, knowing he'd managed to say something when the nurse took to the board again.

"Maybe half a day," it said before the nurse flipped it and wrote another note. "Nice match, by the way. Your avatar looks funny but kicks some serious ass." She smiled as he read it.

He returned the smile, "Thanks. Not so bad for a loss I guess."

The nurse's head jerked back and Rai and Nallie gave him a strange look before they joined the erasing and writing. Then they stopped and thought, erased again and wrote some more. Flipping the board at him again, he raised his eyebrows.

"Loss? You didn't know you won the match?"

Pointing at himself, Luca burst out, "I won? Are you serious? I won?"

Rai nodded with a grin as Nallie flipped the screen to the replay stream. Luca tried to tell them he couldn't hear the feed. Rai noticed and turned on the captioning.

He read the anchor's words, "Luca the Lucky turned out to be very lucky today. After falling behind in the fight, he came out a champ. Here is the replay of the shortest match in arena finals history," as the replay came on the screen.

Some of the camera angles indicated the producers had put lenses in the trees and bushes to catch all the action. Luca watched as his avatar broke the arrow and the bow. Then it showed him kicking the knight, following the avatar's flight through the air ending as it was gored by the top of another tree. Then it flashed back to him kicking the knight from another angle, showing his tumultuous tumble, landing seconds after the announcer came on to say Luca won. Shock spread across Luca's face as they showed the replays twice. He couldn't believe it. This wasn't skill. This was sheer dumb luck.

"Guess I was right about it being the shortest match in finals history," he laughed hard before the pain forced him to groan and fall back onto the pillows, holding his stomach while his body stabbed repeatedly with pain all over with every shake.

Thirty

Quinn grimaced at Sasha, who returned her look with a grin. The doctor felt the tension between them. As he looked from one to the other, he looked at Luca's chart to break the awkward feeling.

"So, I don't see a two-wife situation here, but it appears the paperwork may be incorrect?" his gaze went from one woman to the other again, expecting an answer. When he didn't receive one, he continued, "I don't see anything on the ex-rays or the scans suggesting anything that won't heal with time."

"He can't hear anything," Quinn said. "Is that permanent?"

The doctor grimaced, looking at her sternly for interrupting, "As I was saying," he cleared his throat. "There is nothing to suggest there will be any permanent damage, but I also don't see a reason for the hearing loss, which is troubling. If I can't find a reason, I can't treat it. And if I can't treat it, I can't guarantee his hearing will return." Sasha blanched as Quinn's eyes widened. "It may be all in his head or there may be a cause that hasn't presented itself yet. We'll run more tests later and keep him under observation."

"But what about the arena? Surely, he can't be removed from the competition?" Sasha choked on the words as they exited between her lips.

"Well, I can't say anything for certain, but he may not be returning to the arena with the next group. As I said, we'll keep him for observation overnight and make our recommendations on things like that after the test results come back."

"What will change in the next twelve hours that would keep you from making that determination now?" Sasha persisted.

"Young lady, I don't have hours to sit here and explain all the things I know about the human body and the effects of injuries like this from your horrid arena," the doctor dropped his pen and slapped his hand over his mouth as Sasha gasped, looking around for the cameras.

One didn't speak out against the government in places like this. You could be charged and any charge ensured a negative outcome. The doctor could lose his spot in the hospital and be forced into a career without specialization. Quinn rolled her eyes. She knew the cameras didn't watch everyone and the doctor would only be in trouble if someone reported him, but his and Sasha's reactions amused and bored her at the same time.

"So, what you're saying is, you don't see anything and there is no way to really tell until you've observed him for a while and that can't happen unless you keep him here for a few days and your hope is that everything resolves itself because you can rarely treat the effects of the shocks given to competitors and they often cause permanent damage," her tone was flat and informational and laced with boredom.

"I wouldn't say the doctor doesn't know. He is specialized..." Sasha started.

"Actually, that is fairly accurate," the doctor nodded at Quinn. "And that about wraps this up. Do you want to tell him or do you want me to?"

"I'll tell him. He's used to hearing bad news from me," Quinn said, heading back into the room.

"What can I do to help him doctor?" Sasha grabbed his hand, pleading.

"Just be there for him. Keep him informed. And don't panic." The doctor rolled his eyes. "And try to keep those guys as far away from him as possible." He motioned to the producers and cameras down the hall.

STEPS ECHOED DOWN THE hall and Sasha turned to see the herd of producers and camera operators rushing down the hall. Maneuvering around her, the doctor cut them off before they managed to close a meager half the distance between her and themselves. He spoke in tones too low for Sasha to hear but she could see the discontent on the assistant's face. For a moment, the producer's face flushed and she appeared to have harsh words. The doctor motioned back the way they came and eventually, they turned, heading back down the hall.

"Thank you," Sasha said as he walked past her. "You're welcome. I can't stave them off forever." He said, hanging Luca's chart on the door and moving to the next room.

Sasha sighed loudly and her shoulders slumped as she reached for the door handle.

In the room she announced, "Well, the doctor managed to push the producer's entourage back into the waiting area but that won't last long," she said, flashing a smile as she looked up at Luca.

Quinn was running her hand through his hair, and it took a moment for the scene to register in Sasha's brain. They were kissing and neither heard her. Clearing her throat loudly, Quinn pulled away to see who was there.

"Oh," she scowled. "It's you."

"I know, you two can't help it..." Sasha tried to think as her world spun. "It would be better if you could keep that behind more private doors. I know you like one another and Luca has no interest in me really, but it's hard to watch." She sulked as she dropped into one of the chairs.

"Sorry, what was it you wanted to say?" Quinn said, picking up the board to write.

"The producers are eagerly awaiting their interview and to manipulate the situation, which is why you two should be careful. I know it's been a while, but the doctor only managed to delay them. They will find a way to get back here, and they won't knock first either."

Thirty-One

"There is one thing in our favor, you have extra time. The gap between the arena and the Dome is usually about eight to twelve weeks. Long enough to completely detox and be allowed into the Dome." Quinn wrote it out on the board for Luca to see.

Rai shook his head and chuckled.

Quinn eyed Rai and noticed Nallie looked ashamed, at her feet.

"Well, since we have some time, maybe you should tell me what I can expect in the Dome The tactics I might expect and the way we need to prepare." Luca tried to keep himself from shouting but realized everyone had to move closer to hear him as he over corrected.

Quinn looked sheepish. Rai wouldn't make eye contact.

"Quinn, tell me about what happens in the Dome arena." Luca insisted.

"I can't." Quinn wrote on the board without responding out loud.

"You can't tell me? Would that be breaking the rules? How would they know you told me anything?"

"I can't tell you because I honestly don't know. I remember being told about detoxing our bodies and that's it. I know I made it into the Dome. I know I was supposed to fight in the arena. I remember the pre-events. After that, I remember waking up in the hospital inside the Dome." Quinn started to cry.

"That can't be right. You told me you could prepare me for the Dome. How could you prepare me if you don't remember anything? Why don't you remember anything?"

"I can't answer any of those questions. I don't have answers for you." Tears burned in Quinn's eyes.

Rai had slowly moved toward the door before Luca threw a pillow in Rai's direction, "Where do you think you're going? If you know something, you better share."

Rai spun around, his eyes firing a fierce gaze right through Luca, sending a shiver down his spine.

"There is not a lot for me to add. If either of you want more information, you should talk to Halstead." Rai growled as the marker beat the board, turning it in Luca's direction.

"Who is Halstead?"

"My keeper." Quinn said. "She was my original contact to Pyrious. Now she runs our team of recruits."

"Halstead no longer leaves the estate. I think she's bound to it somehow." Nallie casually threw out without writing it for Luca. Quinn scribbled her words onto her board for him.

"If she never leaves, how are we supposed to ask her?"

Rai grumbled, "I know where the tapes are kept. I could get your rounds from the archive, but I would have to sneak them out. No one outside the Dome is allowed to view them, especially not former fighters."

"Have you seen yours Rai?" Quinn asked,

"Fortunately no, but I have been in attendance at the Dome arena before. I am not sure I should share what I do know." Rai had resigned himself to a corner of the room, slumped more than standing and refusing to look at any of them.

"What do you mean, not sure you should share. Of course you should share." Quinn argued.

"Why, so you can go free? How does that help me? I will still be stuck under Pyrious' control and contract until I die. Enslaved to do whatever he tells me to for the rest of my life. Maybe even multiple lives as I have proven how useful I can be." Rai dropped down to the floor as he spoke. When he was done, he sat with his knees to his chest.

"I didn't think..."

"Hey, I can't hear you. Can someone tell me what's going on here?" Luca intruded.

Quinn waved him off. "I didn't consider anything beyond myself. I am so sorry Rai."

"It's not like any of us would have considered you if we'd found a way out of our contracts." Nallie chirped.

"Hello, deaf person over here." Luca whined.

Quinn grimaced and threw her marker at him, waving him off again. Luca ducked under the covers.

"I know it's not like we're real friends," Tears rolled down Rai's face, but his voice remained steady. "We're a group of kids thrown together by circumstance, just trying to survive. I know we need to trust one another, and we rely on each other, but I am under no delusions of loyalty. I get it. You found a possible escape and while I should be happy for you, even trying to help you, I can't help but think that it's so unfair."

"Oh Rai." Nallie cooed. "It's going to be okay."

Quinn wiped the wetness from her cheeks as she knelt down in front of the small form in the corner. "We should be helping each other because our bonds are stronger than that of friends...at least they are for me."

Nallie sat next to Rai, snuggling into him like a small child would to a parent when they want to be held. Rai obliged and wrapped his arm around Nallie's shoulders. Quinn gingerly placed a hand on each knee.

"Why didn't you share your feelings?" Quinn asked.

"I didn't want to stand in the way of your happiness." Rai looked up at Quinn.

Quinn smiled back. "It's hard to see beyond our own happiness sometimes. I wouldn't want to bring you down off that high either."

Quinn stood, holding out a hand for the Rai. He took it and stood, bringing Nallie to her feet with his other arm as he rose.

"So, about those recordings..." Quinn started.

Luca smiled, "Can I know what's happening now? Hello." Luca waved his hands at them in an attempt to shift their focus.

Quinn walked over to retrieve her marker. "We will work on retrieving the digitals and put together a picture for what the Dome holds." She wrote on the board. "So we have to go now. We will be back with more info."

Quinn kissed Luca, ruffling his hair, "You have interviews to prepare for. We'll be back."

Thirty-Two

"Don't you think if we could only get away from here, there has to be some other place that's better?" Quinn asked.

Rai shrugged, "I guess that's what everybody thinks."

"I don't," said Nallie. "I remember enough before being brought here and sold to tell you no place is really better. Unless being free to choose is better."

Rai and Quinn looked at Nallie. Rai raised an eyebrow and Quinn frowned.

"Sold? Where did you come from?" Quinn asked.

Nallie grimaced, "Oh, from another colony, across the ocean. I was trained in all the ways to please my master from a young age. It's a little like the specializing is here except well, at least here there isn't a chance of starving to death with my specialization." Nallie's look trailed off as her brain twisted herself up in her own thoughts.

Rai shook his head, "I feel like we should have shared our stories before now. I guess that's part of trying to get over trauma and pain. You tend to not talk about it."

"Maybe we should start," Quinn said.

They shared a hearty laugh. Nallie snapped back out of her head and laughed with them, despite not knowing what was so funny.

"Found it!" Rai pulled a drive from the archive. "I can't believe Halstead just let us in here."

"Maybe she knows something we don't." Quinn said,

"Halstead always knows something we don't." Nallie said.

They plugged the drive into the projection screen.

"Play." Nallie said. "Regular speed."

"Nallie, have you watched these drives before?" Quinn asked.

"Loads of times, but I skip the gory parts." Nallie replied.

"What gory parts?" Rai asked.

"Who are we watching first? Rai's are better than Quinn's, on the account of the gruesome injuries." Nallie plopped herself in the chair, curling into it like a cat.

"Nallie, why didn't you tell us you'd already seen these?" Rai asked.

"Because you never asked. Oh, but I can't tell you what is on them. I made promises to my master." Nallie smiled, waving her hand at the projection. "It looks like Rai is up first."

Rai appeared on screen in full leather armor. His eyes were wild and he seemed jumpy.

"Is that me. Where is my fighter?" Rai moved closer to the projection. "And what is wrong with my face?"

"That's withdrawal." Halstead made them jump as her voice came from the back of the room.

They watched as Rai committed unspeakable acts. Killing his opponents with ease. Acting like a crazed man with no empathy or mercy. None of them recognized this young man as Rai, as the man that sat in the room with them. Their protector and sometimes mentor. Then it happened. The opponent was faster but no less crazy-eyed and maniacal. He sliced Rai across the chest and stomach before the guards retrained him. Rai watched as he took his last breaths and the crowd cheered.

"Pause playback." Halstead commanded and the screen froze.

Rai and Quinn were speechless as Nallie giddily clapped her hands.

"Halstead, can we watch Quinn next." Nallie chirped excitedly.

"I would pay good money to have them do to my brain whatever they did to yours, Nallie." Halstead replied.

"It was a simple procedure. Helps me be more compliant. I had issues with training." Nallie replied.

"We could watch Quinn's, but I don't know if she is better served watching the top of her head getting sliced off." Halstead said.

"That part is less fun." Nallie frowned.

"Can we not remember because we actually died?" Quinn was the first to get her wits back.

"No, you dying has nothing to do with your lack of memory." Halstead answered.

"How can I trust that is the truth?" Quinn scoffed.

"You remember things before the Dome arena. And you remember things after the Dome arena. You just don't remember anything once you went into detox. Right?" Halstead stepped further into the room. "That logically says that your untimely demise did not mess with any of your memories."

"What aren't you telling us Halstead?" Rai asked weakly.

"I am not sure I am allowed to tell you what I do know." Halstead replied.

Quinn charged across the room, throwing Halstead against the wall. "You will tell us what you know."

Halstead stared Quinn in the eye, gritting her teeth. Quinn sneered before feeling the sparse form in her grasp. When she felt the tiny frame, she gasped, releasing Halstead and stepping back.

"I didn't realize," Quinn stammered.

"We have all done things we are not proud of doing and we have paid our personal costs. This was mine." Halstead removed her hood to reveal her costs.

Their face revealed a story worse than Quinn could imagine. Her skull was flat and she had many implants, including a robotic eye. Most of the skin that should be on her face was only muscle tissue. No ears sat on the side of her head, just holes and worst of all, it looked like her neck was gone. Just not there and her shoulders were nothing but muscle on bone, visible muscle on bone. She looked fierce and frail all in the same moment.

"What..." Quinn started as she felt Rai approach behind her. "What did they do to you?"

"Did that happen in the arena?" Rai almost whispered too softly for anyone in the room to hear.

"No Rai, this was a result of me agreeing to experiments." Halstead started. "Medicinal experiments, or that's what they called them." She replaced the hood. "Experiments of withdrawal from the medicine that keeps everyone alive. We all know that's a lie. It hastens death through addiction and withdrawal, but it keeps the population compliant and struggling. What you may not know, the thirst for grittier and gorier entertainment is at an all-time high, at least for the rich and bored, and it is the commoners, the feudal serfs, as it were, that pay the ultimate price for that entertainment under the guise of a grand life in the lap of luxury."

"We know that we all pay for the arena in one way or another." Quinn said, recovering from the shock.

"Careful Quinn. I wouldn't want to censure you now. You have Pyrious and that good-looking young man right where you want them." Halstead sneered, making it clear to Quinn how she felt about those standing in the room. "If you want to know more, watch your recordings. Not just the fights but the behind the scenes moments. I imagine the unedited digitals might be illuminating."

"Just tell us what you know." Rai insisted.

"I cannot. I physically cannot. I lost my own bodily autonomy long ago. It was different from the choices you all make but just as real. And it comes with real pain and suffering for me to tell you more than I already have." Halstead bowed her head and strolled toward the door.

"I don't understand." Quinn started but Halstead raised a hand, indicating she should stay silent. Halstead had said her piece as she exited out the way she came.

Thirty-Three

"So, we don't have to make any solid plans yet, but we need to be prepared to brainstorm." Rai instructed.

"Shouldn't we at least have a backup plan?" Sasha asked.

"Your trip into the Dome is already secure." Quinn said.

"Now we have to move onto the second part of the plan. We need to make Warren sick so he will be brought to his guardian, who is Luca." Rai said. "We will focus on that part, so no one gets wise." He motioned to Nallie. "You two work on getting him better."

Rai nodded at Nallie, who rose from the chair and followed him from the room. "Bye all. You've been most accommodating." Rai yanked her out the door.

"I don't know if I will be able to compete. What do the rules say about injuries like this?" Luca asked. Even if he couldn't hear his voice, they could.

"Technically, if you are unable to fight, you go home. It doesn't matter what round it is." Quinn said and wrote. "And maybe that will be what is best. You aren't sponsored and you have put on a damn good show."

Luca watched as she wrote furiously on the board. It took longer for him to read. He wished he could hear Quinn. Her voice echoed the words in his head, but it wasn't the same.

She turned the board to him. "Sometimes, they make exceptions for people like you, just like they're putting together an exception for Sasha. But I can't help you if you can't compete and I am not sure I can help you if you can compete. I have nothing left to bargain with." Quinn frowned.

"Did you find the recordings? Did the digitals give you any new information?" Luca asked. "It might be easier to brainstorm if I knew more about the Dome arena."

A tear appeared in the corner of Quinn's eye. "I still don't remember anything and there is little clue as to what happens in the arena once you're inside the Dome." Quinn's stomach churned as she fought herself mentally. Lying to Luca was what they had agreed after watching Rai's recordings and Halstead's revelations.

"Maybe it's better if you can't compete. Maybe this should be good enough. If you continue the love story, you'll still garner enough Digicreds to possibly raise your station and if Warren specializes, we'll still be able to see one another." Quinn turned away as Luca read her response. Then Quinn handed the board over to Sasha and stormed out of the room.

"She's a good person, trying to protect you." Sasha wrote.

Luca slammed his fists into the bed and grimaced. "A lot of good that did for her. I may be out of commission, and she is stuck with that horrible man. If I can't compete, she'll never be free of him. I now see how there are situations that are worse than death."

SASHA SAT CURLED UP next to Luca with her head resting on his shoulder with Luca's arms wrapped around her. They fawned over one another, sharing kisses and touches as the cameras rolled on the couple. The makeshift press conference only served to frustrate Luca as none of the participants seemed to understand what it meant for him to not be able to hear.

"Can you please write your question on the board," Sasha sounded bored as she reminded the current crew again. Both of them had lost count of the reminders.

"If you don't write it down, he can't answer the question. And if it is a question for me, then it's only fair that he knows what we are talking about in case there is a follow-up question." Sasha explained again, shaking her head as she rolled her eyes.

"Luca, were you excited to hear about the rule change?" the producers asked.

"What rule change?"

"The producers made a recent change to the rules changing how eliminations are handled. Unless the contender is too injured or sick to continue, they now just drop to the previous arena when they lose a battle."

"Oh," Luca smiled at Sasha, touching her cheek gently. "So fighters aren't eliminated until they lose out of the first arena. I like it. I think it will make an interesting twist for the arena. Sasha will definitely make the most of her good fortune and second chance."

"Sasha, how have you been handling Luca's recent misfortune?"

Sasha giggled, "I spend as much time by his side as I can. I know I have to go back to the arena rounds soon but I know he'll be watching. I want to ensure he knows I love him and will be here, no matter the outcome."

Luca read the board then moved it out of the way to give her a deep kiss, "I love you too baby."

The producer snapped and Sasha turned. Luca saw the producer's hand up, calling their attention.

"Luca, your brother Warren has taken ill and is in this very hospital right now. Have you seen him? Do you think he will continue in the arena?"

Luca frowned, "I have not had a chance to see him yet. While I am sad that he is ill, I am happy he is getting the treatment he needs, but I think I will advise him to retire from the arena. He can specialize in something which is much more acclimated to his talents."

"I think that should be enough to clip together." The doctor clapped his hands which shocked Luca, who thought he may have heard the clap. "Time for our fighter to get some rest."

The producers grimaced but acquiesced to the doctor's request. Luca tilted his head toward the doctor as Sasha scribbled on the board to explain.

QUINN SAT IN THE CHAIR across from Luca's bed, watching the interviews over and over as he slept. No one knew she was here and that was the way she liked it.

"They are very convincing," she mumbled as the display shined on the wall.

The night nurse came in and checked his vitals without seeing her in the dark corner. In and out without even a second thought.

Luca stirred in the bed. Quinn knew they wouldn't be back for about an hour. She moved chairs and took Luca's hand, watching as his chest rose and fell rhythmically. She laid her head as close to his as possible and before long found herself drifting.

Something touched her cheek and she bolted upward. Luca's eyes were open and he smiled sweetly at her.

"You should probably be at home. What will Pyrious think?" Luca whispered.

Quinn shrugged and shook her head, wrapping both hands around the hand that was on the bed, allowing him to run his hand through her hair. She grimaced, grabbing the board.

"I think you are a very good actor." She frowned as he read.

"Oh, you know all that is for show. Only one person has my heart, and they sneak into my room late at night to watch me sleep." Luca winked. "It's kinda creepy."

She shoved him lightly in the shoulder and they shared a chuckle.

"It has been a while since we had time by ourselves. How you holding up?" Luca tried to keep his voice low.

Quinn shrugged again and moved to curl up next to him on the bed. Then she scribbled more words on the board. "Hard to get those images out of my head. You're so gentle with her. I can see why the producers and well, everyone else just eats it all up."

"If only there was a way for me to prove that you're the only one I want close. Is there something you might be craving my lady?" Luca whispered in her ear.

Quinn raised an eyebrow and nibbled on his ear before agilely hoisting herself on top of Luca. She smiled at him as he raised both eyebrows.

"I see. The lady wants me to prove my deep devotion for her." Luca started but the last half of the sentence was muffled as Quinn kissed him passionately.

Luca allowed himself to fall into the moment, gripping her at the hips. Without his hearing, all his other senses were heightened. He closed his eyes to breathe her in. Quinn awkwardly fumbled on top of Luca, her inexperience shining through. He smiled, trying not to chuckle so as to not discourage her. He steadied her by gripping her sides, allowing her to get things started.

Luca felt her all around him. With every movement, he felt every twitch, every tensed and relaxed muscle.

Quinn steadied herself by placing her hands on Luca's chest, which caused him momentary sharp pain. He gripped her tighter and allowed her to rock on top of him. The enhanced sensations lessened his staying time and before he could stop himself, he released but she continued to ride, more urgently now. Gently repositioning her, she pulsed around him. A feeling he hadn't experienced before as she pumped him for a minute longer, collapsing on top of him.

Their lips met as he held her tightly.

"That was different." Luca whispered.

Quinn scrunched her face as she swiped him playfully on the chest, a little harder than he'd expected. Luca rubbed the injury and smiled.

"Not bad different. Good different. Very good different. Like nothing else I have experienced."

She smiled as they adjusted to lie comfortably next to one another on the bed. A faint noise hit Luca's ears, and he turned his head to see she was chuckling. Had he heard that?

QUINN'S EYES BURST open. She hadn't meant to fall asleep. It was still dark outside, and Luca's arms were wrapped around her. A smile crept across her face as the door swung open.

The nurse smiled, checked the chart, checked Luca's vitals, tilting their head to Quinn before they turned to leave.

A heavy sigh of relief pressed through Quinn's lips as she squirmed to remove herself from Luca's grasp, careful not to wake him. She leaned over to grab her boots and as she straightened up, Luca was sitting up on the bed.

"I see." Luca smiled trying to keep his voice low. "You're sneaking out on me."

"The same way I snuck in." She said, forgetting to jot it down.

"Same what?" Luca asked.

Quinn froze. "Can you hear me?"

Luca crinkled his nose as Quinn grabbed a board and pen.

"Luca, could you hear me?"

"I'm not sure." Luca said.

"It's been weeks." She wrote then mumbled, "The D ome a rena is dangerous."

"What's ignorant for weeks?" Luca asked.

Quinn raced to find the doctor.

Thirty-Four

"I think it's great that your swelling has gone down and that you are hearing more." Quinn bit her lip tentatively. "But they said you might never regain all your hearing, and your balance could be affected."

"I know, but all I have to do in the Dome is control an avatar, right?" Luca looked at her and smiled. "So there's little danger in it. I just have to train harder."

"It's not that simple Luca. It may be better for you to bow out now. Your underdog status have earned you enough Digicreds that Warren can specialize and move you to a different and better Block. One closer to the Dome. Better life accomplished."

"I don't understand Quinn. Why are you trying to get me to back out now? It makes no sense." Luca said.

"I just worry about you." Quinn argued back. "It's not as safe and easy as you might think."

"Quinn, there is something you're not telling me. Why won't you just tell me?" Luca persisted.

"I don't know if I can. Besides, it may take too long and be complicated for me to explain if I have to write everything down." Quinn said, "And I don't want to write it down anyway."

"So you found information about the Dome arena? You remembered something?" Luca's tone softened.

Quinn frowned, shoving her hands in her pockets and staring at her feet.

"Quinn, look at me. What won't you tell me?" Luca pleaded.

She pulled the chip from her pocket, placing it in the projector. Refusing to look at Luca or write anything else on the board. "Play." She commanded and motioned to the screen.

The playback began to roll as Quinn helped herself to the foot of the bed as a seat, forcing Luca to sit up to give her enough room.

"Quinn, I don't..."

She raised a hand to silence him and motioned again toward the screen. Luca watched as Quinn appeared on the screen, looking crazed and unrecognizable. They watched as she brutally ripped through her competition. No bruising affected her drive. No amount of blood slowed her own, despite it being hers.

As they watched, Luca kept one eye on Quinn, eyes wide with tears in the corners, hand over her mouth to muffle her responses. Shaking her head and on occasion, shielding her face from the horrific events on the screen. Luca felt the same level of horror mixed with confusion.

Then it started. The final match. Quinn looked less driven, more exhausted. She fought arduously but her opponent turned out to be too much. They sat, mouths agape as they watched the side of Quinn's head sliced off, falling to her death. Her last breaths an up close view from the drone cameras. The screen went black and neither moved for quite some time.

Luca regained his senses first.

"Quinn, what the hell..."

Quinn's hand flew up again, silencing him.

"Quinn, where was..."

She waved him off again, but he ignored her. "Where was the avatar? Quinn, what..."

He moved closer and found her weeping. Placing a hand on her shoulder, she didn't shirk it off. Luca held her as she cried. When the tears stopped, she curled up in his arms and fell fast asleep.

"I'M A MONSTER." QUINN whispered timidly.

"You're not a monster. There has to be an explanation for what we saw."

"That's the Dome arena Luca. They trick you into sacrificing yourself. If you go into that arena with no sponsorship and you die..." Quinn couldn't finish.

"You have to talk a little more slowly and a little louder Quinn. I'll have an avatar." Luca gave her a warm look, reaching out to touch her cheek.

She turned away from his hand. "No Luca, you won't have an avatar. This is the Dome arena. Rai was just as crazed, until the end." Quinn tried to explain. "Halstead says it's withdrawal."

"Withdrawal...from what?"

"I don't...Luca." Quinn turned and gripped him by the shoulders. "Do you remember anything from when you stopped taking the pills?"

Luca tilted his head at her. "It's all fuzzy. Not memories really, just emotions." His eyed widened as he realized the horrible truth. "When they say we have to wait to detox, they're not just talking about the pollution on our skin and stuff, are they? They make us go through withdrawal."

"I think they make you fight while you're in withdrawal." Quinn corrected. "I think they do it so you'll fight like crazy and not be able to control yourself."

Luca gulped down hard.

"If you've already gone through withdrawal..." Quinn tried to put the full thought together. "Then you will be going up against crazed monsters. With no sponsorship, when you die. That will be it for you. For us. For Warren." Quinn struggled to keep her tough exterior. "You have to tell them you are not fit to compete Luca."

"But then I'll never see you again." Luca broke down, tears burning down his cheeks as he reached out for Quinn.

But she pulled back, shaking her head. "I'd rather lose you and you be alive than to..." Again, the words wouldn't come out of her mouth no matter how hard she willed them.

They stared at one another. Quinn's chest ached with every breath and thought of losing him forever, but she didn't see another avenue.

"Luca, I think I love you. I want you to be okay." Quinn finally whispered. "If that means we never see each other again, then that is a price I am willing to pay."

"Quinn, I don't want to lose you. I shouldn't have to lose you. This choice is unfair." Luca wiped his nose with the back of his hand.

"It's not really a choice, is it?" Quinn held his gaze, her stoicism quickly returning.

"There has to be another way." Luca pleaded.

"I don't see one." Quinn said. "It is what's best for everybody."

Luca scoffed, "Best for everybody? There is nothing even good about this for anybody."

"That doesn't change the fact that there is nothing we can do about it. Luca, this is our only choice." Quinn said.

"What about other contestants? There has to be something we can do." Luca insisted.

"Luca, you have to be realistic about this. It's not the time to be looking out for anyone but you and your brother." Quinn almost shouted. Stepping back, she turned to regain control of herself. She had to do the logical thing here and distance herself.

"Luca, I don't have the luxury of your optimism. I have to be pragmatic about this." Quinn walked to the door, placing her hand on the handle.

"Wait!" Luca called out. "Can't we talk about this?"

"There's really nothing more to talk about. I have to tell Pyrious you're not able to continue. There are outstanding bets that need to be reconciled." She heaved a sigh as she pulled the door open. "And I have a contract to uphold."

She refused to look at him as she turned. Luca slammed his fists down on the bed but said nothing. The door began to close behind her.

"We have to put a stop to it Quinn. We need to stop them from hurting anyone else." Luca cried out, his voice hoarse.

Quinn froze, sliding her foot to stop the door. For a moment, she considered what he said. Grunting as she turned, she stuck her head back into the room. "What did you say?"

"We have to put a stop to it Quinn. We need to stop them from hurting anyone else." Luca repeated.

The words stopped her again. She hadn't considered this a possibility. Stepping inside the room again. "You need to be careful what you say here in public. You could get in so much trouble."

"We have to stop them. Quinn, you have to help me stop them." Luca sounded more confident.

"But how?" Quinn started, rolling her eyes at the idea she could entertain his altruism.

Luca stood weakly, "I have to go into the Dome arena."

She gasped as he door clicked closed.

Thirty-Five

"Pyrious, we can't send Luca into that arena as he is. He's been off the meds for so long that he won't be affected by the withdrawal. He'll get destroyed in the first round." Quinn protested.

"I see you've watched your digitals. That's against the rules Quinn." Pyrious sounded more sinister than usual. "But I can overlook it..."

"There is no price for me finding out what happened to me. I am looking out for your pocketbook." Quinn tried to sound authentically concerned.

"You don't care about my pocketbook." Pyrious spat back. "I should have you cast out for the way you're speaking to me."

Quinn swallowed hard, "I don't mean to upset you, but we need some supplies to create an adrenaline pill that will give Luca a chance."

"Why should I care? I'm not his sponsor." Pyrious looked her up and down. "Don't think I haven't noticed how much of a shine you have taken to your arena boy."

"That arena boy has brought in more profits than you have seen over the last five years. You're just going to throw him to the wolves and risk the market?" Quinn smiled triumphantly.

"You're much too smart but that's one of the reasons I like you. You're almost my equal in intellect. Now if only you had the power." Pyrious chuckled maniacally. "But that is what you lack."

"Look, you do this and I guarantee the returns. Luca the Lucky returns to the arena, damaged goods and sans withdrawal. He'll be the underdog for certain."

Pyrious eyed her suspiciously, "Show me this list of supplies."

Quinn knew he could not resist a good score. With the amount of money he was making off of Luca the Lucky, he could buy himself the highest status in the Dome. He could become the chairman, a level of control and power he would not pass up.

She slid the pad to him. As he looked it over, Quinn bit her lip.

"The Chemist needs these supplies for what, exactly?" Pyrious asked.

"To produce an adrenaline pill so arena boy will have a fighting chance." Quinn said.

"And then we take the pills away when we want him to lose." Pyrious' creepy grin returned.

"That is the plan." Quinn steadied her tone.

"Guess you're not as sweet on him as I thought." Pyrious gently touched her cheek.

"Well, how could I be sweet on him when I am yours?" Quinn replied sweetly, batting her eyelashes.

"Halstead," Pyrious screamed. "Get her whatever she asks for. Ensure safe passage to the Chemist." He threw the pad onto the table. "Now my dear, let us go celebrate my new found fortune." He wrapped his arm around Quinn's waist, forcing a kiss. "And no, there will be no delay so you can't drug me to sleep this time."

Quinn tried not shudder as he pulled her toward his bedroom.

LUCA LOOKED OVER THE arena, gulping down hard. After making it through his first bout by the skin of his teeth, the doubt of success was creeping into his brain. Rai stood behind him, watching as the previous match was cleaned up.

"Looks like they might be a while. The producers have called for the jesters." Rai said. "That one was brutal."

"I've seen worse," Nallie said as she approached from the side tunnel. "But I've been to the Dome arena before."

"I'm surprised Pyrious let Rai come." Luca said timidly.

"Someone had to be here to make sure you take those pills. Which reminds me." Rai said.

"Thirty minutes ago." Luca answered before Rai could ask.

"You might have to take another dose. Those will only last about thirty minutes." Rai replied.

Luca and Rai stepped to the side of the tunnel as men removed the losing contestant, in pieces.

"There's no resurrecting that." Luca shook his head.

Rai averted his gaze.

"You would be amazed at the med tech in here. Never say never." Nallie's tone was far too upbeat for the circumstances.

"We don't need the details Nallie." Rai's voice was breathy, as if he might be sick.

Nallie frowned.

The jesters filled the arena floor, doing tricks and making fun with the workers cleaning up the remnants of the ruond. Luca found himself smiling and laughing before long.

"It isn't funny." Luca whispered to himself, turning from the macabre sight.

Within a few minutes, the jesters came dancing past them.

"So much for a longer break." Rai said.

"The next match," The announcer's voice bounced around the arena. "Welcome the underdog back to the arena. Lucaaaaaa the Luuuuuuuuckyyyyyyyy!"

The crowd erupted as Luca puffed up his chest and marched out into the arena.

"We will see if his luck holds out against The Amaaaazing Averyyyyy!" The announcer's voice disappeared as the crowd rose to their feet.

Competing chants of Avery and Luca echoed in the air. Luca's hands began to tremble and to quiet them, he released a roar only adding to the cacophony. Scanning the area, a heavy weight hit his stomach as he saw Quinn in Pyrious' box. This was the last thing he wanted her to witness.

The pills were kicking in. Could he take another life for the sake of trying to put an end to this tragedy? He wasn't sure but he would defend himself to the death if necessary. The buzzer sounded.

Avery charged Luca before he could bring his arms down, bowling Luca over.

"Avery," Luca shouted. "We don't have to do this."

Avery pinned him to the ground, eyes wild. Luca pulled his free leg up, slamming his foot with all he could muster into Avery's torso, throwing the big kid off Luca and onto his back.

Luca jumped up quickly. Avery appeared to have trouble breathing. Luca jumped on top of him.

"Really Avery, if you could just pay attention to me for a moment." Luca slapped Avery, leaving a mark on his cheek.

This seemed to snap Avery out of his difficulty, and he pushed Luca in the chest, causing him to fly backward. When he landed, Luca's lungs emptied and he found it difficult to breath. Despite the struggle, Luca scrambled back to his feet, rubbing his chest.

Avery wasn't on his feet yet. Luca approached slowly and carefully, circling around to what he knew was Avery's weak side. Blood trickled across the dirt. Luca froze, disbelief written all over his face.

He could hear the announcer's voice echoing but was too far into his thoughts to know what they said. Luca hadn't hit him hard enough to cause any damage, had he? Peering over at Avery, he saw a flow of blood coming from his nose, but that wasn't enough to pool and flow. Gingerly, Luca stepped closer and that's when he saw it, the deep gash on the back of Avery's neck.

Avery's blades were blade up on his back and unsheathed.

"What was he...never mind, he wasn't thinking." Luca thought as he retraced what happened in his head.

When Avery was knocked on his back, he must have nicked his neck. When Luca hit him, he accidentally induced the fatal blow. Luca bent down to survey the injury and found Avery was still breathing, shallowly.

"FINISH HIM! FINISH HIM! FINISH HIM!" The crowd chanted filling Luca with vitriol.

"I can't feel my legs." Avery whispered tersely. "Just finish me."

"Your sponsor can fix that. But if I kill you, they will own you." Luca pulled out a knife, causing the crowd to erupt around him.

"Better than being alone." Avery coughed. "Please."

Luca placed his knife in Avery's hands and helped him to finish the blow. Luca sucked in hard, concealing his true feelings. As blood dripped from his dagger, he rose to his feet, raising his hands in victory.

"Yeah!!!" He screamed as his heart broke. Luca had made it through round two.

IT WAS EASIER TO CART off Avery than the previous loser, but it still sat heavier with Luca than seeing the previous match. Rai put a hand on his shoulder as Luca re-entered the tunnel.

"Look Luca," Rai leaned close to his ear. "You're plan isn't really working. So, I am going to need you to trust me."

"What..." Luca started.

Rai jumped in immediately, "No questions. Just know this is plan B."

Luca stopped walking, squaring up to Rai. "I'm going to need more than that if you want me to trust you Rai. She's in the arena."

"I know." Rai moved as if to check Luca's ribs, leaning back to his ear. "She will be safe if you trust me and do exactly as I say."

"What do you want me to do?" Luca seethed.

"Let out a roar and push me and Nallie to the cut out by that exit over there." Rai motioned with his shoulder.

Luca looked, seeing the exit, looking at Rai as he pressed his abdomen.

"This man needs a medic." Rai turned to the guard as Nallie ran to brace Luca on one side. One guard was sent. "Sorry Nallie." Rai whispered. "Now."

Luca screamed, grabbing Nallie and shoving her to the ground. She slid toward the exit as Rai grappled with Luca. They tussled down the corridor until Luca threw Rai up against the door.

The guard raised his weapon, "Hey you two, stop it!"

Nallie swept the guard's leg, dropping him to the concrete with a heavy thud. The weapon flew out of his hands. Rai caught it mid-flight. The butt of the gun knocked out the guard. Nallie and Rai rushed to the niche, pulling Luca with them.

"Open your mouth and plug your ears." Rai said and they followed instructions.

An explosion sounded outside, then another, then another and the corridor shook or was were the explosions reverberating through Luca. He couldn't be sure.

Then the chaos started.

Thirty-Six

Quinn walked onto the balcony as the previous bout ended. She looked down the row of executive boxes. The Chairman was a few balconies down with no connecting balconies. Other powerful families populated the boxes around them. Across the arena sat the Dome residents. None of them in power but enjoying all the luxury the Dome could give them. They kept the gambling racket spinning, the underpinning to this entire spectacle.

The jesters were entertaining the crowd by the time Pyrious joined her. Pyrious' son caught him up on the rounds of the morning. Who was in and who was dead. What the racket looked like. Who owed money and who they owed money to, almost shouting over the ravenous crowd.

While she listened closely, she feigned ignorance and watched the match. Watching Luca toil with his inner thoughts as he approached Avery's body on the ground, Quinn shouted "Finish him!"

Then she checked the balconies to the left and right, giving an obvious nod and receiving the signal back. She leaned over toward Pyrious' ear.

"Darling." She whispered.

He swung his hand in her direction, waving her away as he discussed the business.

"Baby, this match is already over. I find myself wanting some excitement." She whined into his ear just sensually enough to catch his attention.

He turned to face her, "You have not shown interest before. What changed?" He looked skeptically at her.

The chanting in the arena grew as more people began to scream her line, rising to their feet.

"I just, well, you are good at pleasure, and I was hoping this match would have more action. The action helps keep me satisfied." She smiled at him and kissed him on the cheek. "Please."

"Well, I wouldn't be a gentleman if I allowed my lady to beg." Pyrious smiled, cupping her ass and kissing her on the lips.

Pyrious' sons groaned. "Dad, go into the suite for that. Don't make us jealous."

Quinn led Pyrious back into the box. From the corners of her eyes, she caught the same happening in boxes all around. She smiled as she shut the door and blacked out the windows.

By the time she turned around, Pyrious had his pants off and had positioned himself on a plush couch, "I knew you would come around eventually."

She had to admit that he was good at making her orgasm, but that only took the edge of the hatred. He hadn't satiated her need to care about the person giving her the pleasure. She tried not to grimace as she removed her undergarments while he stroked himself. Kicking off her shoes, she mounted him.

"This is your first time to ride a man. Am I correct." She nodded. "Then I will help you."

Placing both hands on her hips, he prompted her to rock. "Yes, just like that. Don't stop until I tell you to stop."

Quinn complied with the order. Then he maneuvered her out of her top and instructed her to lean closer. As she did, she heard the announcement of Luca's win. Quinn let down her hair as Pyrious gripped her breasts, moving the nipples to his mouth. She groaned in pleasure.

He pushed her back up, "I may not last long this time. My pills are wearing off." Pyrious cried out.

"I was counting on it." Quinn said as she felt him begin to spasm inside her.

She gripped her hair pin and stabbed him in the chest as she rocked. With each wound, Pyrious released a groan. His sons pounded on the window, indicating they should quiet down. Quinn couldn't help herself. She moaned in pleasure as she succumbed to the rocking motion, stabbing Pyrious to death.

"I didn't expect to enjoy it this much." Quinn whispered with her last thrust, hearing his last breath wheeze out of his mouth.

Quinn dismounted as the music for the jesters began to play and the audience began to clap and laugh. Grabbing her shoes, she removed the incendiary devices hidden in the heels. Placing one on Pyrious' chest and the other in the doorway before exiting. As she raced down the long corridor to the stairs, shuttling other concubines with her, explosions went off on the other side of the arena, shaking the entire building.

Alarms sounded but the inhabitants of the boxes were locked outside on the balconies. The group managed to make it down the stairs amid screams and more explosions. Smoke billowed toward them as they hit the underground tunnel.

Huddling together, low to the ground, they opened their mouths and plugged their ears. Explosions went off above them, one after the other. So close together in time it almost sounded like one large, continuous eruption.

Surviving spectators panicked in the smoke, screaming and running in all direction. Some fell directly off the platforms onto the roofs and floors of exposed tunnels below the seating area. Many jumped into the arena itself, heading for the tunnel openings, desperate for escape only to be met by the competitors being brought up for the next rounds. The fighters' withdrawal causing a blood-thirst normal humans would usually never experience. Spectators found themselves being cut down and hunted by those they had brought into this hell.

Quinn lead her group to the exit Luca and Rai pried open. They ran down the pathway and to the edge of the Dome – the rendezvous point.

Luca, Nallie, Rai and a handful of others waited for them there. Quinn took in the sight of the burning arena, surprised they had blown out half the glass wall nearest the arena's interchange.

LUCA STOOD, TRANSFIXED by the flames and the damage. Maniacal laughter echoed off the wall behind them. They huddled tightly together watching glass chunks and metal drop from the BioDome's perfect curves.

Poofs of flame shot high as the filtered air inside the Dome mixed with all the pollution outside. Luca hadn't wanted to kill anyone and now all the people in the arena...He couldn't wrap his mind around what he had become a part of.

Why didn't Quinn tell him about the plan? Luca knew the answer but refused to acknowledge it. Quinn had proven more calculated and deadly than he ever thought possible. As he watched her approach the rendezvous point, he couldn't stop himself from seeing her differently. Now, he hesitated as she came near, almost like a stranger inhabited the shell he had come to recognize as the woman he loved.

He never wanted this. He could never see Quinn the same. He never thought his arena run would change his world forever. How could he save Warren now? Did they just make things worse? Where were they all headed from here?

"What is the rest of the plan, Quinn?" Luca's voice was flat and even.

"The rest of the plan?" Confusion showed on Quinn's face. "This was the plan."

The words echoed around his brain, sparking something hot wrapping around his neck, choking him just enough to allow the shock to show on his face.

"Luca, are you okay?" Quinn put a hand on his chest.

He stepped back, "Am I okay? With what Quinn?" The words burned on his tongue. "About becoming a mass murderer or resorting to extreme violence and destruction? Did you even consider the retaliation?" Luca was trying to keep his tone steady, but the anger dropped into his chest, burning the emotion throughout his veins. "I can't believe you didn't think this through."

Quinn scoffed, "This was the best I could do on such short notice. Sometimes we don't get all the time we need to set a plan in concrete terms. It's not like your plan to turn 'competitors against the system' was working. Don't take it out on me because now you aren't in control."

"None of us were ever in control, Quinn. Of any of it. None of us have control of anything right now." Luca shook his head, slumping back on the wall away from her.

"This is us, taking the power back." Quinn stood over him, her frame looking ominous with the flames and smoke hovering behind her.

"What power? None of us have power. We will never have power Quinn." Luca released a heavy sigh, sitting in the discomfort.

An awkward silence fell between them and for the first time in a long time, Luca wanted to find comfort somewhere else, with anyone else. Quinn didn't trust him or find him capable of, well, anything. It was a strange thing to see when the proverbial wool is removed from your eyes. Bittersweet at best, but this realization devastated Luca into silence.

"You stupid children." The gravelly voice ripped through Luca as the shock they were already caught fought to take hold.

Quinn gasped.

Thirty-Seven

"Halstead!" Nallie yelled as she raced toward the cloaked figure, arms outstretched.

Halstead raised her arm, forcing Nallie to stop and pout. No one ever touched Halstead.

"What are you doing here?" Quinn asked.

"You are stupid children. There is a reason open flame is not allowed inside the BioDome." Halstead said. "So much so that it's really the only rule anyone ever follows."

"How did you know we would be here?" Rai asked.

"Please! You all think you are so clever. I saw the list of supplies for the Chemist. I eavesdropped on every quiet conversation." Halstead scoffed.

"How..." Quinn asked.

"My ears are robotic. Advanced hearing. There is a reason I always know where you are and what is going on." She replied, waving Quinn off.

Rai looked shocked. Luca eyed them suspiciously.

"So you are the personification of the surveillance state." Luca quipped, surprised at the volume and force of his tone.

"I won't be laughed at by someone as lowly as you." She glared at Luca, but all Luca saw was the turn of a cloaked head. "Excellent job. You made the arena explode. We don't know who is dead or alive. Because you were careless. They will track you down and do unspeakable things to you now."

"No they won't. Everyone on the board and their sons are dead. We assured that." Quinn stepped up defiantly.

"How exactly did you ensure that?" Halstead laughed, shaking her head.

"Quinn killed Pyrious before planting the charges in his box. No evidence." Rai replied.

"Well, well." Halstead replied before bursting into laughter.

The group watched Halstead fall to their knees, laughing heartily, not maniacally. Looking at each other, fear written all over their faces.

Luca recognized the sound. How long had Halstead been amongst them?

Halstead's laughing turned into a coughing fit as they dropped closer to the ground. Quinn was the first by their side, helping them to recover and stand up. The hood fell back revealing them to the group. Luca muffled a gasp at the sight.

"I guess that means I'm in charge." Halstead said, the grin widening. "I can't say what the future holds, but I would like to thank you for your service."

Quinn blinked, her expression shifting from fear to shock. "What do you mean?"

"Although you are stupid children, you accomplished in weeks what I have had in motion for years. I guess being an overseer has its disadvantages when you're trying to strike up a rebellion. Causes people not to trust you."

"I meant when you said that you're in charge." Quinn clarified.

"There is no simple answer to that question." Halstead steadied her breath. "So, I will give you the shortest answer possible. I am the Chairman's only living and declared next of kin."

"What is a declared next of kin?" Luca asked, trying to think of anything else.

"Well, that's when the answer is less simple. I don't think I should explain here. We should return to the mansion." Halstead motioned for them to follow as sirens finally started t blare through the Dome.

Luca watched as the fire suppressant units filtered in from outside the Dome. Cars were not allowed in the Dome. Too much pollution. No one worked during the week of the Dome fights.

Rai pulled him to his feet, forcing him to follow with the rest of the group. Everyone had all been in the arena, stuck in the explosion. As the group ran down back alleys and through buildings, all vacant, Luca tried to get the screams and the explosions out of his head, but the experience was stuck deep in his brain on repeat.

A PITTER-PATTER SOUND started to echo around them as they traveled. Then, there was a flash of light and another loud explosion. The group took cover, except for Halstead.

"What is going on out there?" Quinn pressed her way to the front of the group to confront Halstead.

"That, my dear, is acid rain. You have accidentally seeded the clouds with your little stunt." Halstead explained. "Nothing but thunder and lightning. Get up and keep moving."

"What about the people outside the Dome?" Quinn choked. "You said acid rain."

"Yes, acid rain is exactly as it sounds. It will burn the crops and do a number to the soil. Although, it might bring some needed nutrients to the ground. Could be helpful." Halstead spoke more to herself in Quinn's estimation.

"How do you know all that?" Quinn asked.

"I was a scientist. Eco-scientist. Before..." Halstead waved a dismissive hand at Quinn and walked faster, forcing the group to keep up.

Rai pulled up next to Quinn. She knew he had been listening and watching, like always.

"Halstead, you were specialized?" Rai asked.

"No, I was a scientist before..." Halstead began to wheeze as the pace overtook her abilities. "I cannot explain here. We have to get to the house."

The urgency in her voice caused an exchange of glances between the front of the group. Maybe Halstead was crazy.

Thirty-Eight

Quinn gasped as she walked into the lab. This wing was off limits and now she understood why. Old and modern equipment covered the countertop surfaces and the room looked like it could stretch on forever. The floor had splotches from accidental spills but was mostly gray concrete. No marble in this room. No luxuries. Just basic gray everywhere your eyes focused. A computer beeped across the room and Halstead moved to turn off the noise before moving to another part of the space.

Rai pushed almost through Quinn to approach Halstead.

"What is this place?" Rai asked, his voice echoing around the space.

"That is not the right question." Halstead replied without changing her focus or acknowledging Rai in any way.

"How long has this been here?" Quinn asked, the immenseness of the room making her almost speechless.

"Longer than the Dome itself. This was the original facility to research options when the proverbial shit hit the fan." Halstead turned to Quinn and gave her a sickly-looking grin.

Quinn stepped back. "How long have you been here?" Quinn continued.

"Since it opened." Halstead returned her attention to the work in front of her.

"How old are you?" Rai asked.

"I was the first of the immortality experiments. I refused to risk anyone else for my study, volunteering myself to see what the limits were. No one liked the cost to their bodies at the time. So, it never really took. Now, we focus on longevity and well, reanimation." Halstead's attention never left the work she was doing at one of the stations.

"You created the system?" Luca's voice startled Quinn as she attempted to process the information.

"I didn't create it. What I did just paved the way to it. That and the war, of course, but really, it was probably mostly my scientific work." Halstead sounded defeated or maybe wistful. Quinn couldn't put an emotion to the tone change.

"You sound almost proud of yourself." Rai said.

"Why wouldn't I be proud? We have accomplished what was needed for humans to continue on this planet. We have population control, ecological control and a strict hierarchy needed to keep those balances in place." Halstead heaved a loud sigh. "You would not believe the amount of work my colleagues and I put into this endeavor. This model is coveted the world over. I am the guardian of it and thus, we must set right what you destroyed."

"How do we set it right?" Luca asked.

Quinn watched as Halstead paused, like she was deep in thought. Luca moved closer to Rai.

"How would we put it right?" Rai asked as he and Luca nodded at one another.

"First, we need to see if mixing the chemicals inside the Dome with the environment outside changed things too drastically." Halstead went back to her work.

"Well, it is raining. That is different." Rai said.

"That's my point. I must assess the damage first then decide on a plan of action. I am the one in charge now that you took out the power structure. Stupid children." Halstead snapped.

"Seriously, what are you doing Halstead?" Quinn pressed her harder.

Halstead shook her head. "First, I need to establish the effects of this rain storm you created. Then I need to call in the people who are left so we can decide how to proceed forward. We can't dismiss the progress we have made."

Quinn wondered what progress Halstead could be talking about but didn't want to voice her apprehension as she worked. They all needed the answers Halstead was trying to work out. None of them were qualified to get those answers. As the ideas of the progress the elite had created bounced around her head, Quinn returned to the idea of the chemicals in the Dome causing a rain storm when mixed with the air outside. What was in the chemicals inside the Dome? Did they play a part in the longevity of life inside the Dome like the pills served to shorten life outside of it? Was that the population control these elites had established?

"Why won't you just wait to reanimate the people who hold the power?" Luca asked.

Quinn spun on her heel to face him. That was an interesting question. They had reanimated her.

"Because you blew them up. Their bodies no longer exist. I can't reanimate something from nothing." Halstead shouted, her frustration becoming clearer to the group.

Halstead typed on the keyboard vigorously and waited. Then looked over whatever the computer spat back at her. Nodding, she clapped her hands together, her frustration clearly leaning toward excitement. "Maybe you aren't such stupid children after all."

The words rang in the air suddenly overshadowed by another sound. A single gunshot. Luca gaped at Quinn's actions. Now, Halstead was dead. Her last words being that of approval. Quinn smiled as Rai tackled her to the ground.

Quinn struggled against Rai's grasp as Luca pushed in to assist.

"What was that Quinn?" He yelled, his ears ringing from the close proximity to the gunshot.

"Stop fighting us." Rai huffed. "I think she's lost her mind."

When Quinn was finally restrained, they sat her up against the wall. Her look was fierce and defiant. She spat at them.

"Quinn, what the hell are you doing?" Luca asked. "This isn't you."

She stared at Luca as if he was her enemy. "I wouldn't expect you to understand." Quinn finally muttered.

"I think I would understand. So explain it to me Quinn." Rai pushed himself in front of Quinn.

"It was the only way to save all of us." Quinn said. "It was the only way."

Thirty-Nine

Quinn hadn't uttered a single word since the incident in the lab. Not in her defense. Not to show she cared for someone. Not a single word to anyone. Luca knew she was capable of speaking but for some reason, she refused. It has been so long, Luca found it difficult to recall the sound of her voice.

Looking at her now, stone-faced and silent, Luca did feel for her, like someone feels for a wounded animal. Reaching out to grab her hand, she pulled hers back, refusing his touch.

"Regardless, it doesn't matter. It looks like opening the Dome has had some interesting consequences. We grew our first green plant outside the Dome and when we tested it, it was safe to eat." Luca smiled but the look on Quinn's face didn't change.

"I guess I should get going. You'll be out soon. I just, Quinn." Luca choked down his tears. "I can't see you the same. I don't know if I can reconcile the you I saw that day with the you I've come to know. And I need to move on. This will be my last visit."

It was a bittersweet moment, and he wasn't sure why he was crying. Quinn hadn't talked to him in over a year. They had not shared a meaningful glance or touch since he gave witness accounts against her. Not that Luca wanted to speak out against her, but what she did was cold and wrong. He could overlook killing Pyrious but killing Halstead for no reason? It baffled him.

After a long and awkward silence, Luca rose and walked toward the door.

"Good bye Quinn. I hope you find whatever it is you are looking for." Luca banged on the door, and it swung open.

As he waited to be moved around the cell block, he heard something that shouldn't have broken his heart. On the other side of the door, Quinn sobbed loudly. He knew it was over now because she was just that wounded animal. The woman he had fallen in love with was gone.

Beyond the End

The arena burns everyone eventually. We have all become ashes of the arenas, leaving pieces of ourselves where we fought, being burned alive without realizing it. Through electric shocks to the deaths of contenders fighting on a battlefield they don't recognize or remember. The producers strain at the whims of the elite, worried the board of directors could remove them from their perches high above the fringe, resorting to the violence at all costs. Those contenders who don't stay dead know the slow burn of entrapment, caged birds with clipped wings. A drugged population only knowing the flame of a short wick, living life as best they can under the constraints of always being watched. We all burn eventually. Seems like overkill to keep a person in control to me.

There was a time when I bought into the propaganda, thought the system worked if you worked hard enough. I did everything I could to get into the arenas only to burn right along with everyone else, but somehow, I feel much more singed than most.

Luca tapped the pen on the table as he tried to put his feelings into words. It was important to document their struggle, maybe to ensure we didn't make the same mistakes. He was smart enough to know that writing it all down would probably never make a difference, but he needed to process all he had seen. All he had been through. The heartache was too much to bear alone and writing it all down felt like he was talking to someone about everything. Uncensored. Raw. Real.

Our lives have never been great but the Dome arena burning all those people, changed something for not just us. The people inside the Dome, the ones who enjoyed the Dome for all its perks and luxuries, changed too.

Luca stared at the words. Is this really what he wanted to talk about? Paper and ink was always in short supply, and he really shouldn't waste it. But finding the right words to put on the page was sometimes elusive. Maybe this was as bad an idea as he ever had. Self-scrutiny can be difficult.

Luca wondered what Quinn would say to all of this. It had been a long time since he'd talked to her, let alone seen her. It was good she had outgrown him or maybe he had outgrown her. Either way, the thought was a painful one he wished to avoid.

He shoved the papers into his bag along with the pen and stood up from the picnic table. The sun was warm on his skin, unfiltered. Being outdoors on a regular basis felt nice. Of course, one should never be outdoors for too long, if one can help it. Luca allowed the warnings to jingle around in his mind, forcing a smile.

Sasha and Warren had come over the hill. The brown of the vegetation clashed with the shade of brown in their outfits. The young couple looked happy. Luca approved although Sasha was older than Warren by a few years. Luca felt it forced Warren to grow up a little faster. He loved that Sasha was careful to protect Warren from the dangers and traumas of the world. A capable person who lucked out and found her match.

Luca closed his eyes, allowing the wind to brush over him, remembering all the moments that brought him here. All the scars, physical and mental that lead to everything he had today. When he opened his eyes, Quinn was walking across the field behind Warren and Sasha.

"We found a friend." Warren shouted, waving at Luca.

Luca breathed out hard, not a hallucination. After everything...he had been prone to those. Quinn walked with the same reassurance he had always known, head held a little higher than he remembered. The air of being free; of having choices of where you went and who you were around. He recognized the feeling.

"Hey stranger, long time no see." Quinn cupped her hands over her eyes to block out the sunshine.

"Can't hear you until you're closer," Luca said, gesturing to his ear although he assumed she wouldn't need the reminder.

Quinn increased her pace and sat down on the bench. Luca sat back down as Sasha and Warren walked beyond them into the forest.

"Long time." Quinn bit her bottom lip.

"You're looking well." Luca said as he fiddled with the lock on his bag. "Why are you here?"

Quinn looked affronted. "I can't want to see an old friend?"

"Not when you seek them out." Luca said. "If you run into them by chance, that's another story."

"I did run into Sasha and Warren by chance." Quinn smiled.

"Quinn, chance and you have never existed in the same space." His tone was harsher than he meant it to be.

"You would think after all these years..." Quinn's sentence trailed off as the breeze picked up, pushing her hair into her face. "Curiosity gets the better of every human."

"Wait, you're human?" Luca attempted to lighten his own mood. "I'd almost forgotten."

"Hard to forget when you thought I was one." Quinn's voice was soft, almost timid.

"Why are you here Quinn? The truth please." Luca asked again, looking up at her warily.

"Honestly, I ran into Warren, and he said that you would be open to me saying hello." Quinn said. "But I know how things went before and I guess I was just hoping."

Luca smiled as their hands drew closer on the table. They brushed fingertips as they sat in silence for a long time.

"I don't know Quinn." Luca pulled his hand back. "I just don't know."

X-Evolution First Chapter

Tallin began to stir, groaning. D turned on the flashlight, watching him roll over onto his knees. "Shut up Annika!" he barked.

Annika squealed and fell silent. Tallin chuckled, unsure how he ended up near Annika. This wasn't the first time he'd blacked out and ended up down in the secret tunnels.

"Shush. Annika, tell me what happened," Tallin barked again, gripping his head and searching for the flashlight he assumed was on the floor.

"D happened master. D happened," Annika laughed lightly, sounding almost child-like, accompanied by the patter of her bare feet.

D assumed she was dancing around, acting out the way she'd been trained.

"What do you mean D happened?" Tallin growled.

"D is here," Annika laughed again. "Annika...are you okay?" she mimicked.

Now D groaned. This noise just stopped and now, he'd forced it to start again. Tallin charged the light. D hadn't been watching and when he slammed himself into the bars, the clank caused her to shriek. The portable lamp clattered across the ground. Tallin screamed, trying to recover from the blow as D chased the light down the tunnel. She swooped it into her hand and watched it glint of another pair of eyes, forcing the person to yelp.

Recovering quickly, D moved the light to the floor. "Hello D."

It was Kaya. Another small shriek escaped D's lips as she moved backward in reaction to the voice. Moving too far, she ended up against another cell door where two hands reached out and touched her shoulders. They were cold and small. Turning around, she shone the light on a pair of identical twin teens. Both looked back at her. Their faces gaunt and pale. Burlap rags covered their bodies. They didn't say anything, only reached out as far as their emaciated arms could to reach her. Kaya's fingertips brushed her back. D jumped and headed back toward her pack on the floor.

Tallin stood at the bars now, gripping them. D dared glimpse him through a sliver of light. The snake-like grin formed on his lips.

"Clever D. So, this is your answer to my genetic imperative?" Tallin's whisper sounded more snake-like than ever, making her involuntarily shudder when he spoke.

"No, this is my answer to keeping you away from everybody," D said. "Tell me what's going on with Xayres."

"Tut. Tut now. Don't you know how to harness this power?" Tallin tapped his forehead but D was already trying, and his walls were completely up.

She had tried while he was sleeping but all she could dig up were his dreams. Nothing to do with Xayres. Most of the imagery was disturbing. Part of her wanted to find a way to sterilize her brain but she would have to settle for the manual erase option, if she ever could.

"Tell me about Xayres, Tallin. I need to know," D pressed him harder.

Tallin only laughed moving backward as he did. "I will tell you something if you come closer." D eyed him skeptically but inched forward, almost against her own will. Despite his supernatural control over her movements, she remained out of arm's reach. When she was close enough, she turned the flashlight off. She couldn't look at him, not after everything he'd said and done, not just to her but to all his victims.

"Do I still get my kisses?" Tallin asked.

D lurched back, hitting the wall harder than she anticipated. "Eew! No!" Tallin laughed. "Just tell me about Xayres," she insisted.

"Okay, I will tell you something. A story. I know you'll find it intriguing." Tallin said.

"Do you really have something to tell me about Xayres?" D asked.

"Well of course, but the story first." Tallin insisted.

"Fine, a story first," D reluctantly agreed.

"I promise not to disappoint. Now, listen closely. This story is about a child who was so unlike all the others, it caused a problem." Tallin started.

"Let me guess, I am that child?" D interrupted.

"Silence." Tallin shrieked. "No interrupting. Just listen!" He drew in a deep breath. "You see, each bunker had its place and their specialty, but they were built to work together to create the super soldier. You and I are a part of that program D. But you see, something went terribly, terribly wrong in the third generation of genetic manipulation." He paused only long enough to take a breath. "You see D, the genetic manipulation started causing misfires in people's brains. So most of the older subjects were supposed to be sent to Bunker Six for further evaluation. But I didn't want to go." D picked up her pack and placed it on her back. Checking the direction, she feigned a yawn and turned to leave.

"Don't go! I'm not done yet!" Tallin barked.

"I'm fairly certain I know the outcome to this story." D replied wearily.

"No, you don't. But you'll want to know." Tallin said.

D dropped her pack. "I'll give you a few more minutes."

"Very well. You see D, it was imperative we fix the mistake. Fix the misfire. But when they couldn't, they had to follow protocol." Tallin paused, waiting for her to respond.

"What protocol is that Tallin?" D's tone expressed her boredom as she leaned against the cold wall.

"The protocol was to terminate all test subjects. The order came down right before they sent me to Bunker Six. They didn't know I knew but I was cleverer then than I am now – apparently," he sighed as if reminiscing through happy memories.

"Maybe you just got complacent." D smirked.

"What did I say about interrupting." Tallin seethed. "Now, where was I. Oh yes -Only after the test subjects were terminated, examined and the problem found could they start modifying a new set of children. I imagine that's how you came to be the way you are. However, they did not find a solution, even after a decade and thus made the decision to risk a similar outcome. To minimize the damage, there would be less subjects. When the defect began to show itself even earlier in the process, the order to terminate came down again. But this time, the order was only for the one's whose brains soured...unraveled. Those whose brains split or aggressed or well, I imagine you understand."

"See, I still know the end to the story," D protested.

"No, you don't!" Tallin snapped. "You don't because they lied to you. During the new process, your bunker, your home, took in an escapist or so they thought. In the beginning, they tried to assimilate this escapist only to find it wasn't an escapist. It was another genetically modified child, possibly from another bunker system." Tallin took a long pause. "They couldn't figure out how this child arrived, if they were sent on purpose to assist them in solving their issues. So, they decided to train them. In training an amazing mind and genetically sound body, they created a perfect killer."

"This story really has no relevance to me, does it?" D asked.

"You keep interrupting. It's rude." Tallin whined. "You make me lose my place. Okay, the time came when your leadership decided they needed to kill the child and dissect them to find the answer to their issues with the genetic manipulation. When they tried to kill the child, it lashed out and killed them all instead. They found the child covered in blood."

"This child killed my parents?" D choked on the words.

Tallin released a blood curdling scream. D shrank back instinctively. Then he smiled and continued. "That's when they realized, if they could control the child, they could make it into the most obedient soldier, but they found this child impossible to control. So, they decided to erase the child's memory to see if that kept them more docile."

"A kid killed my parents?" D swallowed hard.

"They weren't your parents, dearie. They were always the scientists assigned to care for you while observing you. Your parents probably didn't even know they were your parents."

"So, I am an experiment." D lamented, hoisting her pack onto her back. "None of this is really new information."

"Of course, you already know. You're better than most but you don't embrace your gifts" Tallin cackled. "If you just allowed yourself to thrive, then you would be so much better at it all."

"Thrive how? I have allowed my abilities to develop. I don't stifle them." D protested.

"You stifle them with your empathy. Your relationships. People like us don't do well with others D. We are better in our solitary states." Tallin moved closer to the bars again, his eyes apparently adjusting.

"You'd say anything to get out of there." D insisted.

"Have you ever wondered why they would erase your memory D? Why they wouldn't want you to have the answers?" Tallin's question hit her where it hurt.

"Because they were still running experiments on me." D answered quietly. "And on my friends."

"That answer is way too obvious to be true. I can't believe you never explored more thoroughly. Sometimes I wonder what they taught you in training." Tallin shook his head.

D couldn't see the motion but she could hear the vigorous shaking somehow. Maybe this was a weaker ability rising to the surface in the dark. She didn't want to think about it.

"Don't fight it D. Just embrace it. Your brain is as unhinged as mine. You insert a fake morality to justify all you do but really, you would be fine leaving all the people to their demise, just like me. You want to hurt those that hurt you. You want to act on the dark thoughts. Just embrace it." Tallin smirked but she couldn't see it. She heard it in his tone.

"I don't have dark thoughts about the people around me. I have dark thoughts about the Nazis." D said.

"Only because that's how they programmed your memories. Only because they implanted those thoughts to guide you. D, they erased your memory because you are the perfect soldier. One of the few they thought they could control if they did it right. But, in reality, if you were to ever remember your past, you would see your brain is just as unraveled as mine." Tallin said.

"You don't know that Tallin. You can't know that." D protested.

"Of course I can. I don't have your issue with scanning other people's minds. You think Doc knows how to shield herself from someone like you or I?" Tallin enjoyed delivering the information and did so with fervor.

D went silent as she clicked on the portable lamp and began walking in the direction Peyton had given her. Kaya stood as she passed but D waved her off and Kaya knew her pleas would fall on deaf ears.

"Don't walk away D. There's so much more to say," the volume of Tallin's voice rose but she didn't turn around or motion or say a word which only upset him further. "I am what happens when the genetics go sour, D. And your genetics are sour, just like the Germans. And when it all starts to unravel," He shouted after her. "I am your future D! I hope you looked closely because I am your future!"

Also by Kenny B.Smith

BioDome Chronicles
Ashes of the Arena

Evolution Saga
R-Evolution
D-Evolution
X-Evolution

www.ingramcontent.com/pod-product-compliance
Lightning Source LLC
LaVergne TN
LVHW041925090826
845145LV00015B/688

* 9 7 8 1 9 4 8 6 4 3 2 2 1 *